PIECES OF PAIN

BRIANNE AUDREY

WRITERS & JUNE PUBLISHING, LLC

Book Cover Design by Nikki Sharp

Cover Art Inspiration by Meadow Mota

Interior Layout and Design by ODDO Creations

First edition 2025

To the little girl inside me,
Still trying to heal,
To my inner child,
This is for you

CONTENTS

Acknowledgments

I want to acknowledge those who deserve the recognition—the select few who pushed me for several years to put my thoughts on paper.

I sincerely thank God and, above all, want to give Him glory for His insightful guidance in transforming this story into a published book.

Poppi, Thank you for endlessly encouraging me to write. Your authentic support contributed to the production of this story. "One day, you're going to publish a book." You were correct. I went for it!

A special thanks to Amber Whiteaker for your endless revisions, honest feedback, and, most importantly, for being a breath of fresh air throughout this entire process. I could not have done this without you. Thank you so much, Amber.

Thank you, Stacy Taylor.

Lorena, Sylvia, Ida, Georgia, Latonya & Chuy, Brandon, my sisters, Alexandria, Mrs. Cano, and

Taylene—Thank you for your genuine support, unwavering love, and kindness.

Ama Chela, I love you!

AUTHOR'S NOTE

Dearest Reader,

What you're about to read may be graphic, disturbing, and painful at times. It was difficult to write and may be tough to read. This story reflects the abuse many survivors endure behind closed doors, where there are no cameras, no witnesses, and no one coming to stop it.

I did not include the chapters involving graphic content for shock value. Those chapters exist because real children live these horrors and often grow up thinking what happened to them wasn't "that bad" for the simple fact no one ever gave it a name.

I'm here to tell you what it looks like when someone dehumanizes a child. This is what it feels like when survival becomes your only language.

To those who have never experienced this kind of pain, it may feel exaggerated or impossible. To those who have, I'm truly sorry you understand this reality. I have taken care to present certain scenes through the lens of emotional truth. Though I have fictionalized names, characters, and circumstances, the emotional scars they reflect are very real.

If you are an abuse survivor of any kind, please know this:

You were never meant to carry what they did to you. You are strong and brave and worthy of redemption from the past pains you carry...know you are not alone! And if a scene is too much, skip it for now and maybe revisit it later. Protecting your healing is more important than reading every page, but know that there is light on the other side of the darkness and sometimes there in the midst of it as well.

This book may be fiction, but the strength it took to write it is not. I appreciate your bearing with me through the valleys so we can make it to the mountaintops. Abuse is a difficult topic, but one we can't completely ignore. If you know someone who is walking this path, be an advocate on their behalf, lend a listening ear, and offer a strong shoulder to help carry them to those who can guide them into freedom.

I don't want to leave you without resources if you, or someone you know, have walked in Annie's shoes. There are advocates available to help, no matter which stage of the journey you find yourself.

- **Helping Survivors**: For those impacted by sexual assault or abuse in almost any situation, this incredible organization offers resources not just for reporting, but also for trauma support, legal assistance, education, and more.

- https://helpingsurvivors.org/

- **ChildHelp National Child Abuse Hotline**: This is an excellent place to start the process of reporting child abuse. Available 24/7.

  - https://www.childhelphotline.org

  - Call 800-4-A-CHILD (800-422-4453)

  - Text HELP to 800-422-4453

- **National Runaway Safeline**: For those who are in a difficult situation, are feeling overwhelming emotions, or simply need a listening ear to offer non-judgmental support and guidance toward potential solutions. Available 24/7. Free services for ages 12-21.

  - https://www.1800runaway.org/

  - Call 1-800-RUNAWAY (800-786-2929)

  - Text 800-786-2929

  - Live chat, forums, and many other resources

are also available on the website

- **Child Find of America**: This organization has an extremely inclusive list of Nationwide Safety Resources including Missing Persons, Family & Parenting Support, Mental Health & Substance Abuse, Child Safety & Domestic Violence, Law & Legal Assistance, and even Financial Support & Basic Needs.

  - https://childfindofamerica.org/resources/national-resources/

All my love, prayers, and support,

Brianne Audrey

Chapter 1

S omeday, I hope to own earpieces designed to protect my hearing in loud environments. I dream of a time when inside voices can finally become a reality in this place of mental anguish. Imagining the possibility of a more peaceful atmosphere where constant yelling doesn't drown out everything else. I look forward to not feeling like I'm walking barefoot across a minefield of eggshells 24/7.

I also wonder if Catarina will ever learn to lower her voice and discover the quieter side of communication. There's hope for change, and I wish for a type of calm to one day fill our space. Catarina only knows how to scream to feel in control. As if volume equals authority.

Living in this house requires my little sister and me to take on the role of meteorologists predicting a storm. Catarina's morning demeanor serves as the barometer, indicating whether the day will unfold with ease or spiral into turmoil.

When she is on the phone, Catarina screams. She raises her voice when she asks us to do something for her, and she absolutely screams when she's mad. Her loudest vocal cord is the only effective way to communicate.

It's dreadful waking up in this house sometimes because nobody's day starts until Catarina says. If she is having a terrible morning, then we all know it. I keep a smile on my face in hopes of not upsetting her. From the kitchen, her slamming cabinets and mumbling about doing everything herself are audible.

Today's weather—stormy. I shoot up a quick prayer. *Lord, give me strength.* Skipping my bubbly self to the kitchen, I turn the corner and reach for a dishrag. I hear her mumbling under her breath. Someone has upset her.

"Do you need any help, Catarina?"

"I cook, clean, and slave around the house. I do it all. None of you would survive without me!"

Laughter threatens to overwhelm me, but I know the dangers, so I stifle it.. I listen to her nagging and start wiping down the already clean countertops. Desperate to lighten the atmosphere, I attempt to make small talk. Her uninterrupted stream of anger drowns out my words. Her absurd dramatics reinforce the rage she holds inside.

What baffles me about this woman is her peculiar, illogical insistence for me to wipe already clean surfaces instead of sitting down. After all, 90% of the time, Catarina's activities fall into the lazy category. She spends the other 10% coercing my little sister and me to do her dirty work! Whenever the courage arises to have a decent conversation with her, she brushes me off, her attention fixed elsewhere.

"Remember to wash that filth off your body so you don't make me look bad today!"

We would never want to make Catarina appear incapable of doing her job.

Today, I must behave impeccably because my caseworker is coming by this afternoon. Harper Perry is friendly, even though she seems to be on a tight schedule. Every few months, I look forward to our brief, three-minute conversations. I eagerly anticipate her visits. They offer me a bit of hope. I want out of this place. I don't know where I would go or what to do, but I dream about it almost daily.

The thought of a life beyond these walls is a bit terrifying, but it brings a flicker of hope. I close my eyes as I shower. Warm water hits my spine, and tilting my head back, I close my eyes and envision myself galloping across the American plains like a wild horse. Freedom dances in my head.

Whenever the opportunity to block out reality comes, I cherish the soothing moments. A world of endless possibilities awaits me. But right now, it is a reality waiting at the edge of my imagination.

I'm toweling off my hair when Catarina interrupts my morning routine.

"You better watch what you tell Harper. I'll know if you tell her anything you're not supposed to." If Catarina's looks could kill, I'm not sure I'd be standing right now. Her eyes narrow with intensity, and her gaze locks onto mine with undeniable authority. "If you even think about sharing anything you're not supposed to, I will know."

The tension in her voice always sends an eerie shudder up my spine. Her words carry a weight that crushes secrets, leaving no room for doubt about the seriousness of her warning.

She lights another cigarette. I am terrified of cigarettes. The smell alone can jolt my body directly into the toilet bowl. The first time she used my kneecap as an ashtray, I learned my lesson. Defending myself from a slap to the face was the wrong choice. I learned to take it. Gut punches, kneecap burns, face slaps—I mastered resilience.

Nicole should be listening to Catarina's lecture with me, but she isn't home from school yet. Earlier today, Catarina checked us out of school early. She took

Nicole back but kept me home. She knows it is more of a punishment for me to miss school.

I know Catarina does this on purpose. I already figured her out. Every time the caseworker comes by to do her visit, Catarina makes one of us walk home from school. Santiago picks up Celi, but Nicole and I have to "figure it out." Catarina's threats only drive home her point. I cannot consider crossing her.

My previous report to a caseworker regarding unfair treatment from Catarina Coyazo resulted in more abuse. It was so bad. I have the scars on my knees and under my chin to prove it, too.

Each day seems to start the same. Today's storm is developing into a tornado.

"Stop being useless in the kitchen. I don't care to know about your day!" Catarina's voice drips with exasperation. "Get ready to go to the store before that caseworker gets here."

The mere idea of accompanying her to the "store" fills me with dread. I know this is no traditional store. The memory of our last outing, where I sat terrified in the back of a police car for the first time, flashes across my brain. Every trip with her is an invitation to a traumatic experience.

"Let's go! I will not repeat it. I said let's go!! And you better wear a hat this time, Annie!!" Catarina screams at the top of her lungs while she grabs her keys and heads out the front door.

The front passenger seat is mine. She has me trained by now. Playing classical music, she drives toward her best friend, Mrs. Corine's, house. I feel bad for Mrs. Corine. Catarina has been doing this to her for so long, and that poor woman suspects nothing.

Drive by first. Catarina's number one rule. Check for cars. No cars means nobody's home. Catarina punches in Mrs. Corine's number. I hear the phone ring as Catarina switches to Bluetooth. Corine's soft voice answers the phone.

"Hello, Catarina. I'm out grocery shopping. Can I call you when I get back home?"

"Of course you can, Mrs. Corine. I was checking to see what you were doing." Adrenaline charges Catarina's voice.

I hope a cop pulls us over and scares Catarina enough to stop her plans. Or maybe someone will crash into us—not bad enough to hurt anyone, but at least sufficient to deter what is coming. She pushes the red button to end the call, and before I know it, we are in Mrs. Corine's driveway.

Overwhelming guilt brushes over me even before the instructions come. It feels wrong because it is wrong! Anything other than this. Kids my age usually hope for a trip to Disney World or a four-wheeler. My current hopes lie in not getting caught for what we're about to do.

Catarina instructs my sister and me. We have learned to do exactly what she says, or pain is coming. We tried that route the first few times. Today, we must use ham chunks to distract Corine's dogs.

The next instruction—take sufficient jewelry without detection. How much is too much? I don't own any jewelry and have never bought it. I have no clue how much this fancy stuff costs. How much more can disappear before Mrs. Corine notices?

I run outside and ask Catarina if we need to take the wedding ring on the nightstand. I make it very clear there is no more jewelry we can see.

"Are you trying to get slapped? Don't ever ask me a stupid question again, or you will not have a phone, you will not have food, and you will not get to shower for as long as I feel like it. So you figure it out." Catarina hisses at me as I rush back inside, telling Nicole to distract the dogs while I grab the jewelry.

I help pick up any evidence of the ham deterrent, and we run toward the truck.

"Corine won't even notice this is missing. Her husband buys her so much junk she won't notice anything you girls have taken from her."

Sitting silently inside the car, I immediately ask God for forgiveness. Catarina is right. Anything *you girls* have taken.

It's Nicole and me breaking the law while she sits innocently in the car. It feels scarier the more I think about it. She clarifies to me that if the neighbors ever call the cops, she will tell them we are the problem, and she is the devoted foster mother trying to love troubled kids.

Catarina doesn't have many friends or people in her life aside from her husband, her kids, and Mrs. Corine. I think this sad, lonely existence stems from everything she has done in her life. The thrill in her eyes worsens her actions against Mrs. Corine. A distinct expression appears when she speaks of someone she dislikes. She can go on and on about the person, too. But that look—it's frightening.

Catarina constantly makes snarky comments. Oh, *you have some balls to talk to me like that. You sure aren't afraid to test me.* She is clueless about how wrong she is. I'm not afraid of her.

Although, once I responded to her with a simple "okay." I got disciplined for days for such a casual response. In her playbook, that form of *testing* warranted the removal of all electronic devices on top of dealing with her hostility.

Living with a narcissist is unpredictable. She can keep her disturbing eyes, and I'll keep my mouth shut.

Chapter 2

We pull away from Mrs. Corine's house, and Catarina's threat scares me enough to force a smile at her.

"Cheer up before I give you something to cry about. I mean it, Annie. Change your face now."

"Are we going to do this forever?" Tears threaten as I spit out my concern.

"Just for being stupid, Annie, no phone until I feel like it. Give me your phone now!" Catarina reaches over to snatch my phone out of my right hand.

I hold on a little tighter. She doesn't grab the phone, but before I can look the other way, her thick palm leaves a stinging sensation across my left cheek. I want to ask her if she had given birth to me, if she would still hit me the way she does.

I know the answer. Chances are she probably wouldn't because she doesn't hit her biological daughter—ever. Her daughter has never even been yelled at.

I grip my phone, refusing to let her take it this time. She doesn't pay the bill. She didn't even buy the phone for me! I had to earn my money during summer vacation to buy this phone. She cannot have it. I always give in, but not today. After all, she is taking it away because I asked her a simple question.

I hear her talking, but I don't know what she is saying. I learned to block her out when she speaks. It works great until she asks me what she just said.

"Just wait until we get home. You are going to get it. And you," she looks back at my sister, "you can keep your phone tonight. You know how to keep your mouth shut." Catarina hisses, and I half-expect to see venom dripping from her coffee-stained teeth.

Our foster mother has a lot of rules. One rule is to turn our phones in each day by 5 pm. On weekends, it is 5:30 pm. Vacation—the same rules apply. We must turn in our phones even when we have no school. She even goes to the extent of turning off the Wi-Fi.

Before we return to the house, Catarina has already instructed me on what I will be cleaning. I must have upset her, because I earned myself the task of scrubbing the walls from top to bottom.

After we pull into the driveway, I make my way toward the house. I consider my bedroom and can feel her following me. Risking a backward glance, I turn to see her walking in my direction. I brush my feet across the floor to press my back against the wall, but she corners me. She is so close to my face I can smell the chips and salsa on her breath.

I always tell myself I am unafraid of her, but this moment has proven me wrong. A string of expletives accompanies her repeated demand for my phone. Catarina fumes, but I don't fork over anything.

I try to slip away until I feel her grab the top of my ponytail, twist my entire ninety-two-pound body around, and toss me against the cold tile floor. A small yelp escapes when my knee hits the hard ceramic surface. I can feel the sharp pain shooting a burning sensation from my kneecap to my tailbone.

It hurts so badly, but I manage to push myself back with both arms and scoot across the floor. Catarina reaches for me, but I try to use my arms to block her punch.

"Do you think you can ask me stupid questions or what, Annie? Your own mother didn't even want you. What makes you think I need to love you? Get up off the floor, you dirty pig."

I feel specks of saliva hit my face. Holding back tears, I maneuver myself up from the floor and regretfully apologize for asking her questions.

"Shut up, you stupid idiot! You are just like the junkie who gave birth to you. Good for nothing!!" Catarina continues to lash out at me as I inch further into my room.

She follows me, narrows her eyes, and turns around, slamming the door on her way out. I hear her march down the hallway until her conversation drifts through paper-thin walls. She is in the kitchen telling Santiago I almost got her arrested, which is far from the truth.

Santiago is Catarina's husband. They call him Santi. I guess it is short for his given name. Santi is a nice man—for the most part. He keeps to himself and rarely makes us do things we don't want to do. But where Catarina is concerned, he always follows her lead.

I lay in my bed and rub my knee with lotion to massage through the aching right above my kneecap. I hear footsteps approaching my bedroom. It is easy to guess who it is by the heavy thumping.

I straighten up and act like I am about to clean my closet. The door swings wide open, and Catarina stands there with her right hand perched on her hip. She holds out her hand, palm up, and asks me to hand over my cell phone. I ignore her request, even though it is more of a command that she spits through her yellow teeth.

"Where is the phone? Santi wants the phone, and he said if you do not give him the phone, you are going to get it."

She continues talking, and I reach into the drawer to grab a pair of socks instead. Yanking them to the floor from my hand, she empties the chest of drawers. She cheerfully tosses the clean clothes to the floor. I spent so much time yesterday neatly folding everything that now sits scattered across the room. She takes less than a minute to destroy my bedroom entirely.

After a few minutes of consistent yelling and slamming of bedroom furniture, Santi comes into the room.

"What the heck is going on?"

I make eye contact. But I stay quiet. I know better.

Catarina yells so loudly, I have no idea what she says.

Santi chimes in after watching his wife lose her marbles. He hugs her and whispers audibly.

"Sweetie, make *her* clean this mess. You, me, and Celi can go get an ice cream."

I don't even care if they are leaving me to go get ice cream together. For once, I do not feel excluded. I am happy I will be here alone because the moment they leave, I am ditching this place.

The clock in my bedroom reads 6:02 pm. I hear the truck start and the door shut. I listen for the second and finally, the third to slam closed. They are all inside the truck and driving off.

I charge my phone and grab the clothes on the floor while looking for a backpack to put them in. I grab a black bag with drawstrings from my closet, and shove everything in along with my school stuff. Cinching up the string, I check my phone. The battery is barely at five percent. I need this phone to charge faster.

In the meantime, I leave it without the worry of someone snatching it and go to the kitchen to get something to eat. Most kids have the liberty of raiding their kitchen pantry without repercussion, but my life is a little different.

Here in this house, they have sensors on any door or cabinet containing food. Almost always, if I open the pantry to grab a snack, Catarina will make me aware of what a fat pig I am. I am not sure what pigs have to do with me. At least they get the leftovers. I'm barely allowed to eat anything.

When the thought of never returning to this place creeps through my head, I open the pantry door. *Ding.* The sensor makes a sudden noise as the pantry door opens. I scan the shelves and grab a can of soda from the corner.

Cracking open the warm, carbonated drink I am not allowed to consume, I take a giant swig. The bubbles in my throat immediately cause a reflex, and I let out an enormous burp. Except this time, when I burp, I don't get swatted across the face for not acting like a lady. Instead, I take in the simple pleasures of enjoying a soda.

The sound of the TV in the media room cuts through my moment of serenity. Is someone here, and I didn't hear them? I walk to the other room and see a commercial showing a Shar-Pei dog advertising products for a pet store. I press the volume button to lower the noise and return to where I left my phone to charge.

After quickly glancing at the percentage, I unplug it from the charger and pull the cord from the outlet. If there is one thing I need, it is to preserve the battery on this phone. My reflection on the blank screen reminds me I won't ever have to put up with Catarina's humiliation again.

She gets a thrill out of embarrassing me. She called one of her neighbors just to tell them about an accident I had. *You won't believe this, but Annie got chased by a dog, one of them huge Cane Corso dogs. Here's the knee-slapper, she pissed herself!!*

Yes, it happened, but it was truly an accident. I was terrified of being mauled by a dog and my bladder had a mind of its own! It wasn't the neighbor's business, but Catarina made it known.

My foster mother could never give me love, not even the bare minimum. Hypothetically speaking, even if I became a rocket scientist, I wholeheartedly believe she would downplay the importance. She has always been great at minimizing accomplishments. Nothing I do is ever a big deal.

The clock on the mantle chimes. It must be 6:30. For the first time, I can taste freedom. My life has been chaotic since a young age, forcing me to grow up.

With foster parents or not, I will survive.

CHAPTER 3

I have never been alone, always following someone else's playbook. Most kids feel safe, comfortable, and worry-free at home. Not me. I don't have a typical childhood. Survival requires creativity. At only seventeen, I know how to survive.

For me, role models are not people I look up to. Instead, I have people I *don't* want to be like in my life. I have to be different.

And I have to stop Catarina Coyazo's abuse once and for all. It's time for me to cut the puppet strings. But if I leave, who will watch out for my little sister? Nicole is younger than me. She does not know this woman like I do. I check my phone to text Nicole. Where did she go while Catarina was destroying my room?

Hey Sissy, are you okay?

I hit the send button. Three little dots appear in a bubble within a few seconds as I wait. The notification banner pops up on my screen.

Call me

I frantically call Nicole. The phone rings maybe once, and immediately, the worry escapes my voice. "Hey Nicole, where are you?"

Nicole sounds out of breath. "I ran to the park when I heard Catarina yelling at you."

"Okay, tell me which park, and I'll come to you. I'm never coming back ever again, Nicole."

"What do you mean, Annie? What about me?"

Her last question pierces right through my heart. "Just tell me where you are, Nicole, and I'll explain everything."

I haven't even told her goodbye yet, and I can already feel my heart shattering into tiny pieces. Nicole shares her location, and we exchange a quick, "I love you."

I grab the backpack and phone charger before making my way to Nicole. Fortunately, she is not too far from this house. The park is within walking distance, so I should be there in less than five minutes. Turning the corner, I see Nicole sitting under a tree. I run.

Acutely aware nobody is chasing me, I race toward my baby sister. Nicole jumps up and gives me the biggest hug. Holding her, I breathe in one more moment of her scent. I look at Nicole and remind her no matter where I am or how far I go, all she has to do is look at the brightest star in the sky and remember we are never truly apart.

"Nicole, I probably won't see you for a long time. You have a few years left before you turn of age. In the meantime, I am going to get a job and go to college to help you get out of this place."

As I tell Nicole my plans to help us both, she breaks down into tears. She lowers her head, eyes glued to the ground. No words come out of her mouth. I remind Nicole this is about helping her find a way out. Forced to remain strong, I reach out to wipe the tears streaming down her innocent face.

"Nicole, you are going to be okay. I will help you, but I must get out of this house first and away from Catarina. Sissy, I don't think any court would grant a seventeen-year-old custody of a minor. I have to get a job, but you know Catarina will take every penny I earn if I stay here. We won't even have a shot at college."

Everything I say is true, but deep down, I don't know if Nicole will be okay. I have never been okay in that house of mental torture, and I am the stronger one.

Nicole looks up and gently nods. "Yeah, I know."

Reaching out both hands, Nicole and I interlock our fingers. I may not be crying now because I want her to think of me as unbreakable, but deep down, I wish I could trade places with her. If I could, I would in a heartbeat.

Time travel is not a skill I possess. I can't switch our birth dates, but I can get a job and become financially independent. Hopefully, I can gain custody of her once I am in a more stable position. My phone buzzes, and Catarina's name flashes across the screen. Frantically looking around to ensure she cannot see us, I reject the call.

"Was that her?"

"Yes, but I think I need to go now, Nicole, because you know she'll call again."

My phone vibrates again. As quickly as possible, I tap the red button to reject the call and give Nicole one more hug before I leave. I toss the phone into my flimsy drawstring bag.

"Call me Nicole, please. Whatever you do, even if you have to borrow a phone from a friend, please try to call to let me know you are okay." I hug and kiss my sister goodbye.

I know I am only seventeen, but I have never had to walk away from someone or something I love. No breaking up with a boyfriend, ending a friendship, nothing—but today, I walked away from my baby sister.

Walking through the neighborhood, I cross the bridge to get onto the main road. San Diego is huge. I have to walk and walk just to get from point A to point B. The Coyazos moved to California less than a few years ago. Navigating an unfamiliar city might be difficult.

Honestly, I do not know where to go.

The setting sun reminds me to preserve my phone battery. Despite my minimal packing job, my legs and back ache. I have some socks, underwear, a toothbrush, toothpaste, and one change of clothes, but my body can't take another mile. Sitting on the sidewalk, I stop to catch my breath. I stretch out my legs, frown at the forming bruise around my kneecap, and tilt my head to admire the campus of the local community college across the street.

College never sounded real to me. It was always a dream beyond my imagination. My mother never went to college, none of my aunts or uncles ever attended, none of my cousins—you should get the picture by now. The offer of a full-tuition scholarship to ANY university in the country mattered nothing to me. I had already made my decision to apply to the nearest college so I could remain close to Nicole. Getting accepted was the least of my worries.

My grades never worry me. Learning truly comes naturally. I love to learn and teach what I just learned. Don't get me started on reading and mathematics. Writing, not so much.

A loud car horn blares as a motorcycle rider pulls out in front of it. Deep pink and purple hues make me aware of how late it is. A neon gas station sign a few blocks ahead still seems too far. Making my way on two feet, I hope some merciful soul will give me a ride to Chasity's house.

Chasity Johnson is my closest friend. I know her address by heart. She is the only friend I can trust with what happens at the Coyazos. I remember the day I first told Chasity about our home life. It was not by choice, I assure you. She came over to the house to work on a project together, and she noticed how Catarina was treating Nicole and me. Chasity didn't ask many questions. Instead, she scribbled her address on a scrap of paper and told me to keep it inside my shoe.

Opening the convenience store door, I make my way to the cashier. I am not sure why I feel scared right now, even though I just walked twelve miles alone and not once felt anything other than exhaustion. I look over to see a woman with her two kids. They seem so happy. It's fair to assume she may think I am homeless, as she snatches her kids close to her hip. I scoot back toward the inner aisle so she knows I am no threat. Oh, to have that type of love right now.

I may look homeless, but I'm just a kid who needs a safe place to sleep for the night.

CHAPTER 4

I feel a warm, light touch on the back of my shoulder.

"Honey, are you lost? Where are your parents?" Huge blue eyes, filled with genuine concern, draw me into an elderly white woman's face.

"Um, no. I am not lost. I am just wondering if..." The lump in my throat refuses to set the rest of my sentence free. Clinging to this stranger's tan parka, I bawl my eyes out.

She lets me have a moment, then wipes the tears from my face. "My name is Genevieve Smith, sweetheart. Where are your parents? Are you okay? Let's go sit in my car and you can tell me all about it. Come on."

The older woman's soothing voice ushers me toward the front door. She leads me to a Lexus SUV parked on the side of the building. As she unlocks the doors, I patiently wait for her to tell me what to do next. I have spent so much of my life following orders, waiting for punishment if I move undirected, that

I linger by the passenger door while she hops into the driver's seat. Her confused glance through the window beckons me to open the door and get inside. The silence is awkward for a few seconds with this kind, but concerned, stranger.

"So, where are your parents? And how old are you?"

My head drops. "I just left my foster parent's house. I kind of just need a ride to this address." The crumpled scrap of notebook paper dangles from my fingers. "I don't really know how far I walked, but I just can't take another step."

Her jaw lands on the floor as she accepts the little piece of paper with Chasity's address from my hand. Shifting into reverse, Genevieve fills the silence.

"Have you eaten?"

I ignore the question, along with the slight twinge in my belly, and tell her about my day instead. As soon as I pause, she repeats herself.

"How about we get you something to eat? What would you like?"

"Um, I...so, I have a sister named Nicole. I miss her so much. She's amazing at pretty much everything she does."

Genevieve barely nods her head and smiles. She knows I'm avoiding her.

A few moments pass and Genevieve pulls into the fast-food drive thru. I have always wanted to try this place. It smelled so good each time Catarina brought it to the house to enjoy with her daughter and husband. She never offered to share with Nicole and me unless I gave her money to help pay for the food. Since I was too young to have a job, I never had money. You can imagine how many times they ate takeout in front of us.

But not anymore. Today, this kind stranger goes out of her way to feed me. Nobody has ever been this nice to me except maybe my junior-year English teacher.

Approaching the window, Genevieve grabs her pocketbook to pay for the order. The worker hands her a brown bag, and Genevieve passes it to me with a smile.

"I hope you are hungry. There's enough food to fill your little tummy up."

I thank God for this warm meal and for a stranger—Genevieve Smith. This woman doesn't even know me and has done so much within twenty minutes of our meeting. She even asked me about my day. While my foster mother found pleasure in making me pay or beg for my food like a dog, this stranger generously fed me. Genevieve is beautiful, inside and out.

Catarina always told me rich people weren't nice. That is so far from the truth. This woman looks rich, and by the boulder on her ring finger, it is safe to assume if she isn't, her husband is. She enters the highway to get across the city faster.

As Genevieve and I pull up to Chasity's driveway, she eases her SUV toward the curb and shifts the gear into park.

"Are you going to be okay, sweetie?" Her eyes implore mine with genuine concern.

I nod my head up and down. Deep down, I feel safer *now*, in a stranger's vehicle, than I ever did with the Coyazo family. Knowing I never have to return to Catarina's house again gives me the strength to open the door.

"Thank you, Genevieve, for your kindness. You have no idea…" My voice breaks.

I step out of her SUV, but before I close the door, she tilts her head and flashes a sincere smile. Shutting the door behind me, I walk up the Johnson's driveway until I reach the front door. I ring the doorbell and look back. Genevieve still looks in my direction.

Her presence there reminds me of the time I went to the salon to get my hair cut. I was eavesdropping and overheard one lady talking to her friend. *If you care about someone, then you should wait until the person you are dropping off gets inside. You're making sure they're safe inside their home.*

Today, this elderly woman proved caring for someone requires no length of time. You demonstrate care by how you treat others. She didn't know me. But she knew she needed to help me, so she did.

My best friend swings her pivot-front door wide open. Chasity greets me with an enormous hug. As I step inside and feel the warmth of her home, I look back and notice the silver Lexus is gone.

"My goodness, how did you get here? Are you okay?" Chasity grabs the only belongings to my name out of my hand. She throws the drawstring bag over her shoulder, and we walk inside.

There is something so peaceful about this home. Chasity's mother, Jill, is a psychiatrist, and her father, Brock, is a firefighter here in the city. My best friend has something I have never experienced—a parent's unconditional love for their child. Chasity gets to sit and eat her fill with people who adore her while I starve for an ounce of my parents' affection. She is a special friend, a unique person, and truly a gift from God. Despite knowing the skeletons in my closet, she chose *me* to be her best friend.

Standing beside an enormous kitchen island, I can't help but picture a massive meal spread across the marble design.

Chasity shouts, her head in between the refrigerator doors. She obviously doesn't realize I'm standing a few steps away.

"Annie, we should watch Desperate Housewives or something!"

A silent, but obvious, giggle escapes my lips. Chasity quickly jerks her head around and gasps.

"Think you could breathe down my neck a little more?"

I laugh at her sarcastic comment as we giggle down the long hallway covered in her photos. I don't know why sadness pierces me, or maybe it's envy. All I see are photos of my friend from birth to her cap-and-gown pictures from our recent graduation. I'm not jealous Chasity's parents love her. I am sad nobody ever loved me.

Midway down the hall, I stop to stare at a picture of a younger Mrs. Jill admiring her newborn baby girl. Chasity turns back to me. My eyes remain on the photo, but she interrupts my thoughts.

"Aw, Annie." Chasity follows my sightline. "That was me and my mom the day I was born."

I let out a fake smile along with a deep sigh as Chasity attempts eye contact.

"I'm sorry, friend. I'm sorry every adult failed you." Chasity wraps her arm around my shoulders.

"It's not your fault, Chas. You should not apologize for something you didn't do."

"I know. I know it's not my fault. But I don't know—I feel bad for you and Nicole." Silence accompanies the rest of our casual walk toward Chasity's room.

Her purple bedroom greets us—easily the largest in the house. Being an only child has its perks. Even though I feel slightly jealous of my friend's picture with her mom, I don't envy Chasity's massive bedroom or any of her fancy things. Settling into an oversized, comfy beanbag, I startle at the sudden knock on the door.

"It's just me, girls. I brought in some food in case Annie is hungry." Mrs. Johnson slowly opens the door and peeks her head in.

I get up to retrieve the plate of food and sit on the corner of Chasity's bed.

"Thank you so much, Mrs. Johnson. This smells delicious."

Though Genevieve bought me an entire burger combo and a drink less than an hour ago, I am still hungry. The steam coming off the pasta tempts me to take a bite. I immediately scarf down the food on the plate, not knowing when my next meal might happen. The piece of breaded chicken oozes greasy goodness over my hands as I temporarily forget there are others around me. The taste of this food is way better than cat food—which is all Catarina would grant me after this kind of escapade. Good thing Chasity's mom isn't

Catarina. Mrs. Jill makes the best pasta with chicken. Hands down, nothing I've tasted compares to this delicious meal.

"There's more, Annie. Don't be ashamed to eat as much as you want. Give me a second. I'll be right back." Mrs. Johnson rushes out, clearly on a mission.

I continue eating while Chasity performs her skincare routine. I did not know there was such an intense procedure one should follow for their skin.

"It's just me again, girls. I wanted to bring in some clean clothes for Annie." Mrs. Johnson has such a cheerful tone as she hands me a stack of neatly folded clothes.

Jill Johnson always treats me well. She feeds me until I am full, always makes me feel welcome, but I have never trusted her enough to tell her about Catarina and Santiago Coyazo. Yes, she is my friend's mom, but she is also a psychiatrist. She has this duty to report even suspicion of abuse or neglect to the authorities. As much as I would appreciate her help, I must remind myself Nicole still lives under the Coyazo's rules.

If Catarina has the slightest idea I told someone about how she treats her foster kids, then Nicole would pay the price. She knows the only thing that would genuinely hurt me is doing something to Nicole.

Mrs. Johnson hands me the pajamas. I bring the clean clothes to my face and take a deep whiff.

"These smell so clean. Thank you, Mrs. Johnson."

Jill smiles at me and reminds me to make myself comfortable. She kisses her daughter on her cheek and tucks her in. She walks over to my side of the bed and tucks me in, too.

"Goodnight, girls. Annie, you are safe here. If you need anything, I am happy to help you, okay?" Jill closes the door on her way out.

The Johnsons have no clue how life has been. Chasity is my friend. I don't think she would ever tell her parents. She promised me she'd tell no one, and I trust her.

CHAPTER 5

The smell of bacon and eggs fills my nostrils as I wake up. Guilt assaults me. I left Nicole. My mind can't help but wonder what sort of punishment method Catarina used on Nicole this time. I wonder if she fed her. Catarina has this awful habit of using food against us when she runs out of her demented disciplinary actions.

Chasity is nowhere in sight, so I walk to the attached bathroom and grab the plastic tube from her sink. I dab minty paste on my toothbrush and freshen up my mouth. A splash of cold water revives my face and removes the crusty eye boogers. I whisper to myself.

"It's going to be okay."

There are so many smiles this morning. It feels awkward walking into the kitchen to cheerful faces—or perhaps I am not used to seeing people happy this early. Chasity sits at the dining table eating her scrambled eggs. Mr. Johnson stands by the coffeepot, pouring himself a cup of joe, and Mrs.

Johnson snacks on a piece of bacon. Her bright eyes reveal tiny laugh lines at their edges.

"Good morning, Annie. Your breakfast plate is over by Chas." Mrs. Johnson points to the empty seat next to Chasity.

I sit and thank God for my warm meal, the generous family allowing me in their home, and my best friend Chasity. Gratitude for a friend like her overwhelms me. I compliment Jill Johnson's cooking by finishing every crumb on my plate. Three over-easy eggs, three crispy bacon strips, and two pieces of toast with grape jam. At Catarina's, it would be impossible for me to eat so much at once without her calling me a fat hog.

After breakfast, both Mr. and Mrs. Johnson call me into their family room. They sit side by side on the sofa, their fingers entangled.

"Please, sit down, Annie. Make yourself comfortable." They speak simultaneously, as if they had auditioned for this moment. I sit in the reclining leather chair, and Chasity joins her parents.

Mr. Johnson reaches within arm's length, grabs the remote, and shuts off the television. Sympathy oozes from his pores.

"Chasity will attend college this fall. We are so very proud of her. Do you have any plans now that you graduated?"

I grin with confidence. I can answer this question because I finally have a plan. It has occupied my thoughts for less than twenty-four hours—ever since I saw that community college near the gas station—but it feels so right. I hardly slept last night planning a way out of this chaos that is my life.

"I plan to go to college, and I can live on campus because I qualify for the room and board scholarship."

Chasity can't contain her excitement as she jumps up from her seat.

"Really? We did it, bestie! We are going to do big things now!!" I love how optimistic Chasity has always been.

"Alright, settle down, Chas." Mr. Johnson chuckles but beams with satisfaction at my answer. At this moment, I think he might actually bear enough congratulatory emotion for both himself *and* my absent father.

I ease my overstuffed self from the comfortable recliner and walk to Chasity's room. Gathering the little belongings to my name, I put them inside a larger tote bag Chasity gave me. It is much sturdier than my drawstring version. She always thinks of others. Last night, Chasity walked into her bedroom with this tote bag filled with snacks, some hand-me-downs, and a black framed picture of us.

We met during our junior year of high school. She is the reason I pushed myself to get good grades for a college scholarship.

"Become someone, Annie. You can't be like them!" Her words articulate the gift of genuine friendship. She always encourages me.

Chasity is not like other girls. She is kind and only ever thinks of others. I admire this girl's inability to display jealousy. She is the epitome of a girl's girl—wanting only the best for everyone.

I throw my head back, and my body naturally falls diagonally across Chasity's king-sized mattress. I stare at the ceiling momentarily.

"Do you think Catarina and Santiago will forever get away with everything they did to us?"

Chasity walks away from her Hollywood mirror to the corner of the bed and gently pats her comforter.

"Sit up. I have been wanting to talk with you about this since the day you told me you were in foster care." Chasity's sympathy is thick, so I sit up and make eye contact with her.

"What is it, Chas?"

She seems reluctant at first. Then she word-vomits.

"I don't understand why you couldn't trust me enough to tell me the truth all these years. Like when you came to spend the night at my house, was it because she would kick you out in the middle of the night? Who does that to a kid?"

Chasity paces back and forth across her bedroom. For a solid five minutes, Chasity shares her pent-up feelings about my situation. Chasity is the only genuine friend I've ever known.

"I'm sorry, Annie. I know better. I shouldn't blame you for not coming to me sooner with this, but you have to promise me you will finish college, get a degree, and do something for Annie!!"

She spells my name out loud. "A-N-N-I-E. Do something for yourself, for once in your life. Your education is something nobody will ever take from you. Please follow through with your college plan!!" Tears roll down Chasity's face. I wipe the wetness from my own, too. And with this, I hug my best friend goodbye.

The Johnsons drop me off at the dorms on campus—the place I will consider home. I already sense I should reconsider college or perhaps adjust my plans. How will I survive? I don't know a single person in this town except for Nicole. What is she doing right now? I ask God to protect my sister from evil, but what I really mean is for Him to protect her from Catarina. That woman is evil incarnate, tormented, and seriously deranged.

I climb up a wooden ladder attached to the upstairs bunk. My dorm room is the largest room I've ever been able to call my own. It may be the school's property, and I might need to share it with someone else, but right now, this is *my* home.

Mrs. Jill contacted the university ahead of my arrival to confirm my room and board provision until the scholarship applications process. The college I am attending is the only one to which I applied. It is the closest college to Nicole. I may not have a vehicle currently, but if she needed me, I could reach her sooner here than if I were across the country.

Lying on my bunk while reading my latest psychological thriller find, I hear a tug at the door. In surprise, I turn to find the stranger who is now my roommate. She is a beautiful blonde girl, very slim, and seems friendly by her smile. For the next semester, we will share bunks in this suite-sized room. I lift myself up and climb back down the ladder. Once my bare feet hit the cold, hard floor, I extend my arm for a handshake with the blonde in the doorway.

"Hi, girl! Are you my roomie?" The blonde stranger's high-pitched voice sounds different from my expectations. "My name is Mitsy Jones, by the way!"

"What a pretty name. You remind me of the actress who sings before every NFL game. You look just like her!"

Mitsy laughs the compliment off.

"Girl, I do not look like no Carrie Underwood, but you and I are gonna be great friends!!" She reaches in to give me the biggest hug. And just like that, I made my first college friend.

For the rest of the day, Mitsy and I help each other unpack our belongings and arrange the dorm room the way we want. Mitsy is very girly, and I can tell her favorite color by the amount of purple within these four walls. It seems my friends have a theme going. I wonder if Chasity is settling in well at her new school.

My stomach rumbles like a bear in a deep cave, loud enough for Mitsy to hear over her music.

"Gee, you sound hungry, Annie!"

I laugh off the secondhand embarrassment.

"I am going to eat these crackers I brought and start writing this paper."

Mitsy turns down the volume on her phone.

"A paper? You've got to be kidding me. Classes haven't even started yet!" She sighs.

"What's that sigh about?"

"Because you are one of those students who starts their homework two weeks in advance. I mean, c'mon, we haven't even met our professors, and you're already starting a paper."

She's not wrong, but is it a bad thing? This paper possesses no professor-imposed due date, nor will I earn a grade, but it is my whole life—my life in pages. I must write this paper well enough to earn the room and board fee waiver.

This scholarship is unique. Specifically designed for first-generation college applicants, it offers enough funding to cover textbook fees, four years' worth of meals, a brand-new laptop, and a little extra cash for school supplies. Out of 2,000 applicants, the college only awards one student this opportunity.

This scholarship is more than money to me. It is the start of a brand new life.

CHAPTER 6

I fixate on the pasty green walls of our dorm room. Very few students enrolled in a university are my age. Most students graduate high school at eighteen. However, since I skipped the second grade, I was almost always the youngest in my academic classes. This allowed me to graduate from high school early. My school also offered an early college enrollment program. At seventeen, I successfully earned my high school diploma and an accredited associate's degree from a local university.

I walk over to the cabinet storing Mitsy's snacks and mine and notice my crackers are almost gone. Rehearsing different scenarios of how to ask Mitsy for some of her jerky strips, I silently cringe. I don't even like meat, but I will gladly indulge if she shares. Embarrassment holds back my question. Instead, I grab two squared saltine crackers and lick off the salt before biting into the stale contents.

"Any progress on your paper?"

I choke down the crackers in my mouth before answering her question.

"I haven't started it. I looked into the requirements, and I want to make sure it's perfect before I submit it."

Mitsy raises a brow and, with a perplexed tone, asks follow-up questions regarding the paper. I explain to her the importance of being awarded this scholarship. Her facial expressions reveal our pasts differ. She cannot possibly understand.

Preferring to avoid conflict, I return to my paper. Trying to contact Nicole is my top priority once I finish this application. I'm not much of a crier. My tears, often hidden, signify long-suppressed emotions. I miss Nicole. Although I have shelter, I will run out of food soon and have no form of transportation to get to her quickly. Still, I have hope I will help my sister somehow. No matter how bleak it appears, it doesn't hurt to brainstorm.

The scholarship application asks only one question. My foster mother consumes my thoughts for a moment. Motherhood comes naturally to most women. It should come naturally. Almost as necessary as the air we breathe. Motherhood is beautiful to most women, but not all.

Catarina fits nicely at the bottom of my imaginary pyramid. Parenting doesn't come with a manual to ensure a child turns out perfectly, but it should include love at the very least.

Catarina and Santiago acquired what they needed to become licensed foster parents. It sounded so nice at first, but I was dead wrong. I understand where the grief from my mother's abandonment stems, but I don't understand how people can willingly take two vulnerable children into their home and treat them like a meal ticket.

Writing in my brand-new spiral notebook, I pen the first sentence about myself. I promptly cross it out until black ink obliterates every word.

Spotting my angry scribbles, Mitsy blurts out her shock.

"Sheesh! What's that all about?"

I give her the side-eye.

"I started the first sentence for the scholarship I was telling you about earlier, and um, it just doesn't sound right."

Mitsy's face contorts in confusion.

"Mitsy, I know we just met, but you and I probably come from polar opposite backgrounds. Writing a paper for a scholarship may not be on your agenda the first week on campus, but I don't have a choice."

"Whoa...hold on there! First of all, about half of the stuff I am wearing is fake, and the other half is stolen."

I am officially flabbergasted. If I were a gambling woman, I would not place my bet that a girl like Mitsy wears counterfeit designer clothing. And I would never assume she's a thief! I notice Mitsy's lips moving as she stands from the oversized beanbag in the corner of our dorm room.

"Why do you look so surprised?" Mitsy shrugs. "I guess I *can* pull off the rich girl vibe!"

For several minutes, maybe twenty, I listen to Mitsy vent about her diagnosis since she was seven. Just great. I ditch Catarina only to move in with a roommate who has an actual, uncontrollable impulse to steal.

I want to ask Mitsy so many questions, but I don't. The obvious ones take precedence in my mind. How long has she been stealing? Is this a problem? Can she really not control it? Is my stuff safe? I don't get why I am so concerned about Mitsy's kleptomania. It's not like I have anything valuable—except my saltine crackers. I am not one to fuss about food, but this is the only food to my name until I figure out a plan to cover my meal expenses. My main scholarship covers fees for on-campus housing and a few other things, but not everything. I have to apply for as many scholarship opportunities as I can. Eying Mitsy, I get up from my comfortable position to snag those saltines—just in case.

"Hey Mitsy, when is the campus cafeteria open?"

"How did you know I am starving?!! It's probably open right now. Want to go with me to check?"

I grab my phone from the bed, and we make our way to get some food. The summer in California is outrageous when you don't have air conditioning or a car. I am too embarrassed to admit I don't have any source of transportation, so I follow Mitsy's lead. We make small talk as we walk through the parking lot from the residential side of campus to the food court area.

Mitsy gestures to the door with the words Student Cafeteria above. Wow! This smells fantastic. The Johnsons fed me well before they dropped me off, but somehow, my stomach gurgles like I haven't eaten in days.

"Geez, Annie!!" Mitsy cackles like a hen.

"I know, I know. I ate some crackers earlier, but..." Before I finish my sentence, Mitsy hugs me.

"Don't tell me. I have been there, girl." Mitsy's voice cracks as her eyes fill with water, and I sense a kindred spirit.

My teaching major suits me better than detective work. Mitsy hides her struggles well. It's a compliment to her. She does not give the slightest impression of a person who comprehends the authenticity of a struggle meal.

On our way back to the residential hall, I learn more about my roommate without asking questions. Mitsy has a lot of, let's say, personal issues. She vents about court-ordered Cognitive-Behavioral Therapy to help treat her compulsive spending habits. She maxes out her credit cards, then closes the accounts. Money management isn't her jam. I will just chalk it up to not understanding how to live beneath her means. She also does not need to steal. Like stealing mascara from the corner store because she did not want to spend her last five dollars. Or taking the pen from the desk in the lobby. Again, there was no need for the pen. She just takes things.

Also, everyone on this campus should be thankful this girl doesn't have a podcast, because Mitsy has something to say about everyone! While secretly annoyed by how much my roommate talks, I pay attention to her words. At first, I think Mitsy Jones talks so much she doesn't realize she is rambling through her stories. But I'm not sure that's the case here. As I listen to this girl, what she says tugs at my heartstrings.

"I'm sorry for talking a lot. You're honestly the only person who hasn't told me to stop talking in forever."

Wow, it hits me—Mitsy talks so much because she desperately wants someone to listen to her brokenness.

Chapter 7

I have no choice but to finish this scholarship paper today. I meet the criteria needed to be eligible, and Mitsy is nice enough to let me borrow her laptop.

She shares her first piece of helpful college advice as she types in her password to give me access.

"Always print your essays after you submit them, just in case."

I open the word processing program and look down at the paper containing a summary of the written essay requirements. The scholarship essay prompt is to write about someone who positively impacted my college experience. Even though my foster mother popped into my head earlier, the actual answer is simple.

My *nonexistent* mother.

Despite her absence, she positively impacted my college experience. As an adult, I have to seek a relationship with the woman who gave birth to me. A child teaching her mother how to be a mother—so quaint!!

Saying I am grateful to her for positively impacting my college experience is an understatement. I want to brag about her lack of parenting skills so much I could almost write a novel. Unfortunately, the essay requirements limit the page number to only two.

Do you know how much credit this woman deserves? More than a newly published book, considering she held the power to teach me survival skills without her physical presence.

Have you ever taught someone something without ever being part of their life? Well, Gina did it. My mother exceeded expectations. How could I not applaud her? I'm not applauding a dog for knowing how to bark.

Before she abandoned me, she had the audacity to demand my respect—from the child she discarded for a hit of heroin! I will remind her repeatedly that even a dog can give birth!

CHAPTER 8

Eighteen years earlier.

Santiago Coyazo is the best man in existence. He has patience with my rage. He cooks, cleans, does everything for me, and works daily from 6 am to 6 pm. What a man I married! Catarina Coyazo knows her manipulation feeds his pity. He wouldn't dare ask her to lift a finger in their house. As a matter of fact, when she tells him to jump, he asks, "How high?"

A woman may direct her husband, and sometimes a husband will influence his wife's actions. Then, there is a rare breed like Catarina—she demands. Demands a partner's love even when she doesn't reciprocate. She demands her husband's time while failing to offer a single second of her own. His attention must be on her, even if her focus falls anywhere else. Santi loves her, and he *really* loves it when she uses his nickname.

Nobody in his family knows *her* real name, though. She prefers Catarina over the name her mother gave her. That name is a secret she will never reveal. A simple glance into her past using public resources would likely expose her, and she won't take that risk.

Fortunately, Santiago Coyazo lacks the intelligence to use a search engine. If he knew who she really was, he would have listened when everyone told him to stay away from her.

Catarina picks up a framed wedding photo and lets her mind wander.

They met thanks to her ex-husband. Santi and Dwayne Lou were business partners. They dedicated their time going from house to house, offering gardening services. If hired, they'd tackle the job together and split the earnings.

Dwayne was the worst of the worst. His affair was not her breaking point. It only took two beers before the shoving and slapping began. A few more drinks meant fists connecting with her face. Unfortunately, it took a few black eyes and a lot of heartbreak to leave Dwayne for good.

When Catarina met Dwayne, she was young—maybe nine or ten years old. Their moms were friends by choice, finding commonality in the daily indulgence of alcohol. Their thirst for the sauce surpassed parental duty. Eventually, as a kid, she got used to it. Complaining stopped, and questions remained unanswered. That was life with an addict.

Her mother was not a drug abuser or anything of the sort. Her addiction was the legal kind, and she never abandoned her kids! Still, she and Mrs. Lou, Dwayne's mom, would drink until one or both blacked out. Every. Single. Day. And Dwayne—let's just say birds of a feather flock together.

Meeting Santi, Catarina fell in love with his clean lifestyle and trustworthy nature. She tempted him many times before they dated, even with Dwayne around. He was too drunk to even notice half the crap happening, anyway. While Dwayne nursed the bottle, she would press her body up against that honest man standing across the room. She even went as far as leaning in to kiss him occasionally, but Santi rejected her advances—well, most of them.

The day she finally left Dwayne, Catarina met Santi in the dollar store parking lot. He grabbed her and picked her up. They kissed for the first time. She knew he was the one—it was like a movie scene.

But the fairy tale didn't last. Santi was so naïve. He would never figure it out. But he didn't have to. Catarina's best friend, Gina, was the culprit who finally let the cat out of the bag.

They were all drinking and having a good time one afternoon. So what if they were young—Gina was a fool. She should have known better than to open her fat mouth.

Catarina snaps back to reality as the glass in the frame cracks under the pressure of her grip.

It's not like I forced her to drink with us. She just couldn't keep her lips from flowing as freely as the alcohol. Just watch. I'll show her what happens to someone who thinks they're better than me. I'll never get over it—and her daughters will pay.

Catarina's plan is very simple. She will do whatever it takes to get custody of her best friend's kids. Gina has three of them and one on the way now. She cleaned herself up for them, too. Gina is an exceptional mother. Catarina still claims they are best friends, and probably will for a long time, even after this is all over. She will never feel guilty for her feelings toward Gina—even the ugly, terrifying ones. Especially when another woman is a threat to the appearance of her parenting skills.

Gina is probably a better mom than Catarina could ever be to her two kids. Jealousy sparks deep in her core. She is jealous Gina is smarter, has a rich husband, and, to top it off, she is insultingly prettier. Gina is the only brunette in their small town with green eyes. *It is time to dim the light in those eyes for good.*

It takes only a short time for Gina to become addicted to a popular injectable drug. The entire town knows what she did. They can't stop talking about it.

Apparently, Gina's mom, Sally, had to pick up the four kids after someone discovered them practically living inside a store. An employee found the girls inside the dressing room. When she questioned them, they said they were just trying on clothes, but the same employee kept seeing the four girls around the store for long periods during school hours.

Eventually, a manager called Child Services to report them. Store camera footage revealed the actual conditions in which the girls were living.

Catarina should have felt bad for them, but she didn't. They would not be going through this if their mother loved them enough to get sober instead of chasing her next hit. Gina handed over her parental rights after refusing addiction treatment. *Their mother is not worth a cup of cold soup. Since she's too out of it to stop me, her kids will finally pay for their mother's loose lips. I don't know where Gina's older two daughters ended up, and I don't care about them. They understand too much anyway. It's the younger ones I want.*

It is their own mother's fault for choosing drugs over her own flesh and blood. She is the worst mother ever. I didn't give her the drugs—I just made sure she was in the right place at the right time. I know where she came from and it was easy to send her back. Catarina's lips mimic a Cheshire cat. She is never the one at fault for anything.

Chapter 9

W hen Gina's mother returns to town with the kids six years later, Catarina's plan gains traction. Finally able to interact with the kids, she begins her finest act of manipulation thus far. She will start with Annie's unwavering loyalty. That girl believes anything Catarina says because she was her mom's best friend. It automatically gives her clout.

The first time they visit, Catarina promises to be Annie's mom.

"I understand what it's like to miss your mom. Your mom and I were best friends, you know? That kind of makes me like your mom, too. Would you like me to be your mom?"

Annie looks up at her with a glimmer of hope sparking in her eyes.

"But what about Grandma Sally? Isn't she supposed to be my new mom?"

"Oh, don't worry about her. She has a hard time taking care of you girls because she's getting so old. I'm really doing her a favor and just helping her out."

Sally was strict, but she was strict because she loved those girls more than anything. *My mother never loved me like that. I can't stand back and let Gina's daughters enjoy everything I never had.*

Over time, Annie learns to trust Catarina. She believes the half-truths covered in syrupy sweetness. Occasional candies and treats snuck into her palms don't hurt either. Catarina is a master at her craft—Annie doesn't stand a chance.

There is a dark side to spending time in Sally's care—Annie's uncle. Only Annie really knows when it began, but over time, her mother's best friend earns her trust. While confiding in each other one afternoon, the girl reveals the ticket to Catarina's grand plan. Annie vents to her new mother figure about her uncle's late-night visits and wandering hands.

That information will serve Catarina well, but not because she cares about helping the kid. Catarina wraps an arm around the young girl's shoulders. Though her actions show affection, her words plant seeds of self-doubt and shame. *She must forever blame herself.*

"A man only goes as far as a woman allows him to, Annie. Never forget that!" Catarina's voice takes on an unnatural tenderness as she turns the girl's face toward her own. "If you were loved, you would have a mom or dad to protect you."

Tears well up in Annie's eyes.

"Can you really be my mom for real, Mrs. Catarina?"

"Of course, dear. I can be your mom, just like I promised. I'll even take you to Disneyland! Would you like that?"

Annie perks up, her baby blues widening into shimmering pools. She is full of hope and desire for excitement. *This is so easy! Just a few more empty promises and she'll be begging to come live with me.* Catarina watches as a flash of wariness crosses the girl's face. Annie is too intelligent for someone her age.

"You will need to do something very important, Annie. Do you think you can remember what I tell you?" Annie's chin bobs up and down. She's right where Catarina wants her. "I would hate for you to be separated from your sister. Think of what your uncle might do if you're no longer around!"

"Oh, no! I have to keep her safe! Can she come live with us, too? And go to Disneyland?" Annie's devotion to her sister is stronger than anything. Now that the frog is in the water, it's time to turn up the heat.

"Absolutely! You just have to be sure NOT to tell your grandma what you told me about your uncle."

"But won't that be lying? They taught us about the ten commandments at Grandma Sally's church, and they said not to lie." Her candor is irritating.

"Do you want to be taken away from Nicole? Do you think she will survive your uncle? If you want to stay together, you have to tell the police your grandma knows everything...even though she doesn't. Do you understand?"

Catarina doesn't want to frighten the girl just yet, but she needs to understand the seriousness. She can call the cops enough to get them to investigate, but Annie must do her part. It's the only way this plan works in Catarina's head. *I need to get those girls taken away from that lady and into the system. Maybe I need a backup plan, too.*

Usually, they'll trust a child's account more than an anonymous tip from an adult. So, Catarina alerts the authorities a few times, enough to put the kids on their radar. Then, she calls Grandma Sally and works that angle. She knows Sally will believe her, especially with proof. Of course, there is no actual evidence since Annie did nothing wrong.

During school hours, Catarina pays Sally a visit. She can't have Annie there to eavesdrop. Sally takes great pride in her reputation with the church and the local community. Any threat to ruin it is a personal affront in her eyes. Catarina is simply concerned about Annie.

She is certain the girl ate "special" brownies at the church with some of the older kids last weekend.

Sally is shocked—as she should be. She is *deep* in her faith. Gina is alive right now because of her mother's prayers. But Sally believes Catarina when she tells her about Annie's indiscretions. She casually mentions her granddaughters are going through a lot. The woman is too frail to take in and raise two girls. Catarina reassures her of the wonderful job she's doing with such troubled souls.

It only takes a few more fabricated stories about Annie to convince Sally she can't handle the girls. Catarina calls the authorities several more times and sends them over on false accusations as well.

Her hatred for Gina makes her blood boil. Making her pay is not enough—her children should, too. *How clever I was to send that man back into her life. I knew it wouldn't take long before she was hooked deeper than in the old days. With her out of the way, it's just a matter of time before her children are mine.*

The foster care agency also receives several calls from Catarina as a concerned citizen. She knows the truth. She knows there is no abuse—at least not from the grandma—but that little girl won't keep the secret for long. So, she spreads more rumors—a little truth sprinkled in with the stories should do the trick.

If enough people suspect a child is enduring *that*, someone will visit.

Sally never knows what hit her. The agency officially removes the kids and places them in a temporary foster home. As their very concerned advocate, Catarina plays the part of the shocked family friend well. She will do anything she can to help.

Catarina doesn't feel an ounce of remorse the day she discovers her plan succeeded. It is richly satisfying. Filled with pride, she crushes the system. She found the easiest method to take Gina down completely—*her kids*.

The coming years hold so much promise. *Hello, easy street!*

CHAPTER 10

T he years spent plotting and manipulating are finally reality. *Getting custody of those two parasites could make a significant financial difference for Santi and me. Two checks for them, plus a cash allowance for food and housing.* This is all the motivation she needs. The agency is only eight miles away. The GPS calls out each turn as Catarina dreams.

Oh, to travel again and bite into a fast-food burger if only Santi agrees. She may have to stretch a few stories while trying to convince him to go along with everything, but that is something she has mastered. Santi believes her oldest daughter is Dwayne's. Dwayne could have destroyed Catarina in court, taking away her rights, but they agreed on shared custody instead.

Dwayne has never questioned Jen's DNA, either, and until he does, the truth remains locked away. Telling him the baby inside her womb was his, knowing full well it was Santi's, didn't bring Dwayne back from the arms of another woman. Her storytelling got her nowhere with Dwayne, but with Santi, it is different.

He may lose the little respect he has and hate her for it if he ever finds out. The risk is uncomfortable. But she'll die with this secret unless she's forced to reveal it. Until then, her lips stay sealed. He won't fight her on the plan, either. It's a good one that will benefit their family. How could he disagree?

The parking lot is small, but Catarina pulls into the closest spot to the entrance door. Concerning physical activity, her obesity speaks for itself. Her deceptive charm doesn't come from her body. She uses her heart to prey. Even though she attends church and reads her Bible when she remembers, she doesn't pray *for* people. Rather, her focus is preying *on* people. She preys on her best friend's two kids right now, like a tiger stalking a gazelle. Deep down, she knows her heart is rotten. *If someone could read my thoughts, an asylum would be my next stop.*

Catarina walks into the "orphanage agency" office. She chuckles at her clever, yet obviously accurate, renaming of this official government organization. If a kid does not have parents, what are they called? Exactly.

Approaching the reception desk, Catarina senses immediate irritation. With a fake smile, the woman behind the counter asks if she can help with anything.

"Of course you can help! I would like to become a new parent for the orphans."

Her smile vanishes into a scowl.

"I am sorry, ma'am. We do not use that word here. They are foster children. I suppose you would like to become a licensed foster parent. If so, I will need your state-issued driver's license to schedule you for fingerprinting."

Catarina reaches into her purse to hand over her license. The receptionist continues to type and do whatever she does on her computer. She returns the license and inquires if Catarina might have a few moments for a brief interview.

"Interview?" Confusion clouds her expression.

"Yes, before I can give you a new parent application package, you must pass the initial interview process." She signals to the door, "If you want to come through here, I will set you up on this computer."

I am not tech-savvy and didn't graduate high school, but that will not stop me. How hard can this be?

Catarina clicks the big green tab in bold letters, **Start Here**. She looks over the summary of questions on the computer screen. The first section of interview questions is obvious: name, date, the basics. She completes that section with no problems and selects the next page tab.

Reviewing the next set of questions forces her to spend considerable time on this section. She must manipulate the answers to the set of questions regarding her education, experience, and background. She purchased a false GED from Santi's professor friend from a university somewhere back in Pennsylvania. Of course she meets the minimum education requirements. She can show them the paper with her name on it if they ask. It's not like they will know. She paid top dollar for it to look legitimate.

After what feels like an eternity, Catarina finishes lying her way through this pointless interview. She approaches the exit, activating the button to open the door. Walking to the front desk, where a line has formed, she waits. As her turn arrives, the receptionist announces her unenthusiastic congratulations. The provisionary foster parent application approval already came through. Catarina acknowledges her words with a smile, secretly pleased her custody goal draws closer.

Between Santi's car payment, the rent, groceries, and bills, they do not have enough to eat from the dollar menu even if they wanted to. But tonight, Catarina is ready to celebrate. Even with the long hours Santi works, they still struggle with finances.

Catarina paid her car off last summer with a well-timed lie to her sister. Telling her they were in debt to the IRS and at risk of jail time if she didn't pay them tugged at the right heart strings. *For her to have graduated high school and not me, I think I am way smarter than her.* Her sister believed her, forked over the cash she asked for, and, to this day, has never asked for a cent of the money back. Her sister is a better person than Catarina, that's for sure. She used the money to pay off her car, which eliminated a monthly payment. Every little bit helps.

Catarina pays the fee to enter the parking garage for the title loan company. She rarely pays for parking, but she knows she will be at least a few hundred dollars richer within thirty minutes, so the seven dollars for one hour is not up for debate.

Catarina signs the papers without reading the fine print. No one has a clue what the word APR in bold letters at the top of the loan document stands for anyway, and she does not have the time or patience to ask the lady to explain it.

To keep her loan a secret from her husband, she tosses the paperwork in the waste bin on her way out of the building. She calls in an order for her family at Joe Bob's Seafood and Steakhouse because tonight they are celebrating one step closer to getting custody of Gina's kids.

Catarina tosses in bed, listening to the agonizing sound of her husband snoring. *I wish I could sleep like he does.* Sleep eludes her most nights. *Perhaps all the bad stuff I've done has finally caught up to me, and my conscience won't let me get a peaceful night's rest.* It has been this way for as long as she can remember. She stares at the blank ceiling for hours until her eyes burn. She plots the different ways getting Gina's kids will benefit her.

Her job search these past two years yielded nothing—won't have to keep looking now. Catarina silently hopes the paperwork and training process moves swiftly so she can start getting paid. *The first thing I am going to buy myself with my first paycheck for taking in those orphans is going to be a large pepperoni pizza. And I am going to eat it right in front of them so they can see what the reward is for staying on my good side and doing everything I tell them to do.*

She knows trouble follows these kids. They have never really had an active parent in their life. Gina has been an addict since they were little, thanks to Catarina. All four kids have different dads, too. The thought of how broken these girls are and how easy it is to manipulate them makes her giddy. *Gina made this so easy for me—without even realizing it. My plan for revenge is coming together perfectly.*

It didn't take long for Gina to slip back into old habits with her choice of drugs. She and Catarina used to get high together in their younger days. She cleaned herself up for the first few kids, but, thanks to her so-called best friend, that didn't last.

Now, Catarina can get paid to take in Gina's kids. She can use them to do her dirty work. She has the power to manipulate them into stealing and to dictate their actions. After all, they are powerless unless someone can confirm her involvement. And if they do snitch, she won't have to worry. Who are they going to believe? The kid with a troubled past, or the loving foster parents who welcomed two kids with no future into their home?

Catarina rearranges their trailer to accommodate the girls. She doesn't want her kids sharing their rooms, but she must show the agency case worker no favoritism between her kids and the orphans. She will not go out of her way to buy them toothbrushes, shampoo, or other items, either. The agency must deposit their check into her account before she purchases anything.

CHAPTER 11

Present day.

I grab the sticky note pasted to the door of our black mini fridge, admiring for a moment how pretty Mitsy's handwriting is. She left me a note in cursive black ink.

Have a great day! Left for class early. Use my laptop to check to see if you got the scholarship. Password to login is Hotdog123.

One moment, I love her handwriting, and the next I laugh while shaking my head at her quirks. Mitsy Jones is growing on me. She has experienced more devastation than most of the students here. She does a surprisingly good job of hiding her past and any pain she may have.

I also learned Mitsy is in a sizeable financial hole because of credit cards. She told me she spends hundreds of dollars on her clothes and her makeup just so people will think she comes from money. I question her logic, but that's her explanation. She once shared the way people treated her was based on how she dressed. I completely ignored every word she said after that. I have no clue how this girl even got into college with such flawed logic and reasoning. At least Mitsy is easy to get along with. Now that I think about it, maybe she stole someone's scores, turned them in as hers, and that's how she got into college. Ha! Totally joking.

Unlocking Mitsy's laptop, I successfully enter my credentials to access my student account. I read online they usually email students with a congratulations letter when they award them with a scholarship. No unread messages show in my inbox folder, so I refresh the page. An email pops up from the Department of Education. I read nothing further than, *Congratulations, Ms. Annie Smith! You have been awarded the First Generation Scholarship...*

I am in shock and utter disbelief!!! The scholarship is mine!!! Despite struggling through the instability of an inadequate foster home, this time, I paved the way for the next four years. Guaranteed!!!

The rest of the day breezes by. I attend my classes, and on my way back to the dorm, I stop by the dining hall to grab a bite to eat. The menu here always comprises five different options. I choose the shortest line and eat whatever is served. Pickiness is not an option. I once heard "beggars can't be choosers." I grab my tray and look to see if Mitsy is around. Failing to see her, I make my way back to the residential hall.

I have no other friends, so unfortunately, I depend a lot on Mitsy's companionship. We are always together. She is my closest friend. I haven't told her much about myself, but she seems to care about me. When we are in the dorm and free from homework, we typically lie on our bunk beds and scroll through social media on our phones. We may not speak a word to each other, but it is the best time spent together. I hear the front doorknob tugging as Misty unlocks and swings it open.

Mitsy can get into a bar if she wants. Most of the local clubs are eighteen and up. The majority of our classmates are at least eighteen, so Mitsy has no issues making new friends. They have gone out a handful of times to clubs and nearby bars. I can't tag along even if I want to. My state ID clearly says I am a minor—seventeen. And, I am way too much of a "goodie two shoes" to inquire about a fake one.

I have never been to a party, a club, a bar, or any of that sort, nor do I have the urge most freshman in college get to use or abuse their freedom. To make things slightly tougher for me, I am a virgin in college. Mitsy talks about all these boys she is getting it on with, going out to lunch with, and here I am nodding in agreement like I even know what the heck "doggy style" means. I know it relates to sex, but that's about it. Just four years ago, I was still playing barbie dolls with Nicole, so intercourse is not a topic I care to talk about. Actually, sex grosses me out. It brings back memories I'd rather not recall.

I feel a slight tug on my arm. Surprised, I discover the girls I have seen a few times across the hall. One girl's high-pitched voice cuts through the chatter.

"Hey, girl! We're your neighbors. We wondered if you and your roomie want to come out with us to tonight's concert?"

Mitsy walks out of the bathroom in agreement to count us both there. I don't complain or question anything. We smile at the girls standing in the doorway, and they go on about their business. My stomach flutters with excitement.

I haven't decided what I am wearing tonight, but it won't be heels like the rest of the girls. A stack of clothes rests on the end of my bed. My loan funds haven't arrived yet, so I can't purchase a small dresser like everyone else has in their dorm rooms. This university is not for people like me. They charge for drawers in the room you already paid thousands for, and they charge for parking, and they charge for the air you breathe—okay, maybe not that far, but if they could, they probably would. Unfortunately, I depend on student loans and credit cards to get me through the semester. I even applied to a few job listings nearby. Hopefully, someone will give *this* teenager a chance.

Mitsy's closet has more variety than mine, so I take her up on the offer to borrow anything from her wardrobe. Mitsy is the fashionista, but picking an outfit is easier than expected. I choose a plain, black, knee-length, spaghetti strap dress. The decision against heels made, I slide on the only somewhat-cute sandals I own.

"Yes, queen! Yesss!" Mitsy snaps at me with a sassy tone.

I hate receiving compliments. I don't mind giving them, but somehow God gave me a roomie who thrives on complimenting others. Since the day we met, she has shown me she is a *girl's girl*. Dressed in our best, we hit the streets!

The concert is out on the campus lawn and filled with students, sweat, and deafening music. The DJ plays Fergie's "Glamorous," and the crowd goes wild at the throwback sound. Everyone screams each letter at the top of their lungs.

As I embrace the ambiance, I feel an ounce of guilt stab my chest. Nicole is living a nightmare, and I am out here having the time of my life. Amid the obvious guilt trip, I grab my phone and dial Catarina's cell.

I see a long, skinny arm reach over and pull my phone out of my hand before I hit *send*. What in the world is this person thinking? Who even does that? The lack of respect in my generation is almost as nonexistent as my parents. I look back, not surprised. It's Ditsy Mitsy. I snatch my phone back out of her hands, and Mitsy glares at me.

"We did not come out to this event, *so you can be on your dumb phone!*"

I respond with an eye roll because she is right. It is my first time out, and here I am, trying to be sad. I put my phone's ringer on silent and click the little moon icon that shifts it to Do Not Disturb mode.

Nothing is going to stop me from feeling normal tonight. For the first time in a long time, I don't feel the need to survive the moment. I am not in a fight-or-flight state of mind, either. I take a moment to enjoy the normalcy of freedom.

At the young age of seventeen, I have experienced more than a teenager should have to endure. The pain stems deeper than my parent's abandonment. Rooted so deep, it transforms into resilience daily. It surprises people around me to discover I am genuinely a kind person. I'm nice because life has not been nice to me. I freely give the love my heart desperately seeks.

Chapter 12

I start my first job today. While I feel grateful to have a source of income now, this is the knee slapper—my first day of work is my birthday. On the bright side, now I can afford to eat whenever I want. I think my roommate caught on to me. Last night, Mitsy asked me what kind of pizza I craved for dinner. I was too embarrassed to admit I couldn't afford to split the cost of a $7 pizza right then, so I told Mitsy I was not hungry.

"I didn't ask if you were hungry. I asked what kind of pizza you wanted, because I am buying! It's my treat, so hurry and tell me what toppings you like before I order you the kind with pineapples and mushrooms."

We both laughed about that, and eventually, I told Mitsy I preferred my pizza topped with cheese only.

My new job is pretty laid back. I work at a restaurant across the street from the university campus. It is also my first job. I will train this week and, depending on how well I do, I will get to work without a shadow next week. Not too shabby for a seventeen-year-old!

There is a big difference between me and other kids my age, mainly because they are still in high school. Catarina would not permit me to take a driver's education course in high school, either. That was another weird rule she had. She allowed her biological kids to take Driver's Ed but never gave a second thought to enroll Nicole and me, her foster kids, in the class.

I learned the hard way, thinking I could outsmart Catarina. It was my senior year of high school, and I voluntarily registered myself in the forbidden course. Surprisingly, this woman, who did not have an ounce of education, caught onto me much quicker than I anticipated. Despite her lack of book smarts, she was always ten steps ahead of me.

I thought I got away with it until one night we sat down for supper, and Catarina decided everyone at the table, but me, would eat that night. The smell of sizzling chicken wings still makes my mouth water. They ate hot wings while I watched. I remember Nicole's face that night. She couldn't eat her meal. But Catarina, Santi, and their two kids? They probably ate a dozen each with absolutely no remorse.

I kept thinking back on every word I spoke to Catarina that day. Did I say something wrong to upset her? I could not figure it out until I physically noticed the evil within her. The memory still sickens me.

She reached over to Santi's plate, grabbed a chicken wing drenched in hot sauce, and chucked it directly at me, striking my upper right cheek. A bloodbath of sauce covered the table, dotted the walls, and splattered the floor! Nicole stared at her in utter amazement.

Catarina walked to where I sat and violently tapped my forehead with her index finger, punctuating each word she spoke.

"You think you are so smart taking that driving class behind my back? Well, you sure are going to learn something today!"

I won't forget the look on her husband's face. Ever. He looked at his wife with no concern or reaction. That man was *used* to his wife's fits of rage and was obviously comfortable with her irrational behavior. Maybe at that point he mentally clocked-out. Who knows?

The front door lets out a loud chime as a customer enters, dissipating the smell of hot wings drifting from my memory. I kindly inform the young lady we are closing soon.

Now that I have a job, I can ask Mitsy for a ride to the Motor Vehicle Division to apply for a state identification card. My boss informed me this afternoon I need to give him a copy of my driver's license, but unfortunately, I need a car to take the exam. A state ID is all I can get for now.

I reached out to my foster mother to request my birth certificate, social security card, and the paperwork needed to obtain a valid driver's license, but she didn't care. Instead, she cut me off mid-sentence and told me if I had funds to buy a car, I should also have enough to pay someone to help me get a license without the documentation.

Catarina's thought process lies in stark contrast to mine. She thinks like a criminal—because she is one—while I strive to approach life logically, intent on avoiding that downward spiral.

I never want to become a reflection of Catarina, so I ignore her hateful comments. I'll get a valid license somehow. And one day, maybe I'll become a caseworker who sees through the façade of negligent or unfit foster parents. My heart aches for each child who endures the trials of this broken system. I hold a special place for them in my core.

Too often, I use humor to cope with unresolved trauma, and the car situation falls under that category. Before the end of my shift, I tidy up the place and ensure everything is ready for the morning crew. My co-workers are all ready to clock out for the day.

My manager, Bryce, grabs a tray full of what appears to be perfectly edible pastries and tosses them into the plastic bag he is holding. He crinkles his right eyebrow and hesitates, almost like he is afraid to speak to me.

I break the ice because I am not one to beat around the bush.

"Can I have that bag? It's empty, right? I mean, it doesn't have trash in it? Like, it's just the empty bag with the pastries you threw in there?"

Bryce pauses me with the palm of his hand raised up. I shut my mouth and immediately regret what I just asked. His facial expressions lie somewhere between confused and *girrrllllll whaaaat*? I don't know how to address this man who is probably in his mid-twenties or early thirties. I don't know if he would take offense if I put Mr. before Bryce, but I also don't want to give the impression I am too young to understand respect. These are the minor issues inside my head that trigger anxiety.

Bryce walks over to the front area of the restaurant, shuffles through the paperwork on top, and then reaches into the drawer. He shouts from across the room.

"Give me just a second."

"No problem." I wait in the same place I was before he walked out.

My co-workers have all left, so at this point it is just my manager and me. After a few minutes, he walks in and hands me a blank, white envelope. He just hired me today. This couldn't possibly be anything too big. Bryce's voice shifts with a touch of sadness.

"Please, do not open it until you get into your car. It is dark outside, and it is dangerous to carry any amount of cash on you."

I say nothing and just nod my head up and down in agreement at his request. I squeeze the envelope tighter with my hands.

"Thank you so much, Mr. Wellington."

"Please, just call me Bryce." I guess it is safe to assume he is not *that* old.

Now that I am an adult, I am not much of a hugger, so I don't give him any sort of handshake or hug to show my appreciation. I just use my words to thank him.

Back when I lived with Catarina, physical affection was an expectation. Catarina's husband, Santiago, would exchange Wi-Fi privileges for foot and leg massages. A twenty-minute massage meant twenty minutes of internet connection. Plus, the physical stuff got Nicole and me leniency.

"Annie, you ready to clock out? I'm fixin' to shut everything off." Bryce holds the door open for me.

I don't have to walk back to the dorms tonight, on my birthday, in the dark, after a long shift on my first day of work. I appreciate the ride more than Bryce knows or can even imagine. After being on my legs all day, I was not looking forward to the walk back. It feels good to know I work with wonderful people. I thank Bryce for the ride and for the envelope, too. He acknowledges me with a thumbs up and reveals a row of perfectly white teeth.

I walk up the metal stairs and press the elevator button because I am up one more flight. Tonight is not for exercise. The elevator beeps as the doors open. I turn and wave at Bryce. I assume he is still looking in my direction, but it is too dark to detect any movement behind the front windshield. He flashes his Mazda's lights.

I meander down the hall, taking a moment to thank God for what I have accomplished in just a few weeks. I graduated high school with enough credits to earn my associate's degree, and now I am enrolled at a university.

Today, it's my eighteenth birthday, and I can say I have my very first job! I am living a life I once prayed for. I used to pray to God on my hands and knees to give me the courage to get away from Catarina. Knowing I stand on my own two feet, something she told me I could never do without her, makes me so happy.

Catarina outright refused to provide any documentation needed to verify my identity. She withheld my birth certificate without a valid reason.

Even more frustrating, she kept the money I received as gifts from people like the Johnsons, the pastors from our church, and my biological relatives who generously sent contributions for my future. She withheld it all.

I left with absolutely nothing, not a single cent to my name. But I'm thriving without her. Happy Birthday to me!

CHAPTER 13

"**S**URPRISE!!!!!!"

My eyes scan our small dorm room and recognize two or three people out of the bunch. What the heck is going on? Did I just spoil the surprise for someone else by walking in right now?

Before my intrusive thoughts flood my brain, Mitsy grabs my arm and yanks me to the side by the bathroom, cheerfully letting me know the surprise is for me. I can't get away with telling her today is my birthday. I like my roommate. This girl is me in so many ways.

"Now, let's get this party started, Chica!!" Mitsy introduces me to practically everyone inside our dorm room. Being in a sorority has helped her quickly make friends.

For the rest of the night, instead of proceeding with my plan of lying down and reading a new book by my favorite author, Mitsy teaches me how to shotgun a White Claw. Apparently, that's what college is for! Most parents think their kids have to go to college to succeed. I beg to differ. Within the last few weeks of attending this university, I witnessed at least three people drop out of their courses, use up their student loan limit, and are now on a daily alcohol binge.

The sad part is one day it will hit them like a ton of bricks when they find out they still have to pay back all that money they borrowed, even though they didn't continue their education. Having no sense of self control at a young age sure is a quick way to jeopardize your future.

It is true, drunk people say it all. After everyone went back to their dorm room, Mitsy and I laid in our bunks, tipsy, and swapped traumatic experiences.

Mitsy found everything I told her about my life with the Coyazo's so upsetting, but she freaked out when I mentioned my inability to use the internet or my phone when I wanted to. Just when I thought I could not trauma dump more, I share life details with Mitsy I have told no one before.

It sucks admitting things people my age experienced normally were never part of my upbringing. I missed out on parties, going to homecoming and prom, the adrenaline rush of sneaking out of my parent's house, and being able to talk to my mom about a crush on a boy. Instead, I had to do whatever Catarina told me to do just to attend school events with my friends. I even stole a present one time for a gift exchange at school—I either stole like Catarina demanded or got a beating for disobeying her. I made excuses to avoid stealing, but Catarina always insisted on her way.

Nicole and I had to wake up and clean before we left the house. Every morning, we were up before dawn because Catarina was slamming cabinets loud enough to wake the neighborhood. Nicole and I had to get up while her biological kids knew they could continue sleeping.

The foster care agency used to give us clothing vouchers. Catarina would take her kids, Nicole, and me with her to the store, but we didn't get new clothes. We had to share the little she gave us with each other while Nicole and I watched her kids fill their baskets with clothes, shoes, and even a backpack one time. She said nobody would ever believe me if I opened my big fat mouth. I always thought if our caseworker had only looked at the receipts, she would have seen Catarina had used the vouchers for her biological kids.

It's the same with the GED she claims to have earned, but I know the truth. She falsified those documents to become licensed. I am not exactly sure who she bought it from, but she purchased her GED. She did not earn it. If she did not have that minimum education background, I do not think she would have qualified as a licensed foster parent. I mean, what example could she possibly give a child in need? No wonder she couldn't help with basic math homework, especially multiplication.

I once asked Catarina for help with my homework. Her response showed her own ignorance. "You'd be lighting the fuse to my tampon, so don't you dare ask my help for your stupidity." I'm still confused by what she meant.

Mitsy bites her nails so badly I can see the blood dripping from the side of her cuticles. Her fingernails, which were once polished in a pretty, dark red color, are now completely bare.

"Dude, you have to write a book because—I am so sorry to say—but this is freaking crazy!"

If she only knew the half of it.

The surprise party was fun, but reading a book would have been better. I prefer to avoid the spotlight any way possible. Reading is my favorite hobby.

I learned to read the dictionary on my own so I could discover the correct pronunciations and definitions of words. With so much knowledge that comes with reading, I immediately fell in love. I'm still smitten with the way each page smells and how a crisp new book brightens the smile on my face. Reading helps me escape from reality.

I needed that escape so many times. Catarina had an odd way of disciplining Nicole and me. Nicole loved the outdoors. On days Catarina felt like it, she would pull open the blinds, have Nicole sit down, and order her to stare out the window. Catarina would crack open the door and ask Nicole questions.

"Hear them kids out there on their bikes having fun?" Then she would laugh like a psychopath.

Kneeling on the gravel rock in the backyard was Catarina's idea of a lesson after I tried to tell the CPS worker what was *really* going on. I did my best not to move. If I did, I immediately anticipated a stinging wet rag lashing across my back.

It is sad to think about it, but my foster parents were never exactly parents to Nicole and me. They fostered us to collect a check.

I will do whatever I can to help Nicole get out of that place. Contacting the authorities is a risk I cannot take without being in the same home as Nicole to protect her. I already alerted them twice, resulting in beatings.

To keep Catarina from touching Nicole, I would tell her to hit and punish me instead. If she felt the urge to discipline my sister, I would volunteer in her place. Every. Single. Time. Sometimes, a big sister must sacrifice herself.

The big blue skies remind me of the bright parts still inside Nicole. She is like a delicate flower—quiet and beautiful. My baby sister is the smartest, most caring person I know! Most girls her age are not sweet like her, either. I hope the world's unkindness and unpleasant experiences don't callous her innocent soul.

Nicole is a person I will gladly peel an entire pomegranate for. I text those exact words into my phone's notes app.

I am not as worried about Nicole. She is doing a great job of borrowing her teacher's classroom phone to call me every day. The first time she reaches out, I tell her to make it a daily thing, even if it is just to let me know she is alive. She understands the importance of keeping in touch. I take some comfort in Nicole's word that things are okay at Catarina's. I don't know that for sure, but I know my sister is *not* a liar. While I have to trust my teenage sister's words, I fear she withholds some truth. Maybe she doesn't want me to worry. I could be wrong, but my intuition says otherwise.

I think of the different things Nicole must be doing right now.

Forced scrubbing of the toilets.

"Every time you flush that toilet, you better have the bottle of bleach in the other hand, ready to scrub!"

Pulling weeds outside barefoot in three-digit weather.

"You can choose to pull weeds barefoot for one hour, or you can keep your shoes on and pull weeds until I tell you to stop."

Personally, the one-hour barefoot was always a no-brainer. Poor Nicole isn't as sharp with Catarina's manipulation tactics.

I look down and take a moment to thank God for the shoes on my feet. When Nicole chose the option to keep her shoes on, I didn't think it would be that bad. I mean, yes, I assumed Catarina would have been mean about it, but the way she made Nicole weed in the blistering heat from sunrise until the moon came out at night was excessive.

She wouldn't allow Nicole to sit down, and I honestly can't say for sure if she got water that day. I spent most of it bent over on my knees eating the meatloaf I had spit into the bathroom trash bin earlier. Catarina made her special meatloaf for breakfast. Who gave it the name *special meatloaf*? And who serves meatloaf for the first meal of the day? It was the closest thing to canned cat food a human could consume. You know, the kind packaged in a little aluminum dish? It smelled and looked just like that, down to the same consistency.

Anyway, Catarina made her meatloaf recipe, and I just couldn't eat it. Warm milk was not enough to wash down the ketchup-filled, watery beef contents. I thought it was a brilliant idea to wipe my mouth with a napkin, spitting the nasty concoction into it each time. My napkin was way too full to keep hiding in my hand under the table, so I got up to slip it into the bathroom trash bin without thinking about it. I returned to the dinner table, and, no joke, less than thirty seconds after I sat back down, Catarina was in the bathroom, screaming her head off that I was going to get it.

Catarina had to put others down to make herself feel superior. Belittling me, in some twisted way, elevated her own self-esteem. Like any other parent, she could have just spoken to me about why I spit out my food or possibly even just let it go because it's not that big of a deal. But Catarina *had* to escalate the situation to make sure she maintained control. She thrived on harsh criticism. It was her way of asserting dominance. A child should never receive such severe verbal disapproval from an adult. It is not right.

There was one time Catarina was not too harsh. I had intentionally done my makeup badly. Honestly, I looked like a clown. I did this to prove a point because I started guilt-tripping myself into thinking maybe I was losing it. Even though I asked Catarina how my makeup looked, I knew she was going to say she liked it.

She did not just tell me she liked the makeup, though. Catarina Coyazo's face lit up like it was the

Fourth of July. She almost jumped out of her recliner to tell me how much she *loved* my makeup. She knew my eyebrows looked like I drew them on with a Sharpie marker and my lips were so over-lined I could give a duck a run for its money. Somehow, making myself look awful was the first time I ever heard a compliment come out of Catarina's mouth.

Aside from that one occasion, my efforts to put on makeup or dress up never garnered commendations. If I looked rough, I knew she might share some kind words with me, but if I ever got ready and made myself look pretty, I can't recall a single time she told me I looked beautiful. It hurt a bit more when her daughters, Jen or Celi, dressed up or had their makeup on, and Catarina complimented them in front of my face. It stung to see the way she loved her daughters openly.

She always seemed embarrassed by Nicole and me. Her narcissistic tendencies left me feeling overlooked and deepened my insecurities. The more I yearned for a mother's love, the deeper the dagger pressed.

I don't need Catarina in my life for anything, but I do feel connected to her while my baby sister remains in her control. A young college student with no permanent residence means it is almost impossible to request custody. And who am I kidding? I can't move my teenage sister into the dorms to live with me. Still, it would be easy to sneak Nicole onto campus and not let her leave, keep her quiet, or whatever, but it would raise issues if we were to get caught. Also, the cops would be involved, since Nicole is a minor.

After I everything I just told her, Mitsy would be cool with it and would even go as far as helping me hide her in our room if we had to, but I do not want to destroy all our futures by teaching Nicole to do things the wrong way. The easy way may offer a temporary solution, but taking the simple route often results in a heftier price paid in the end.

If I want Nicole to live with me and know she is safe, I need to get a place of my own and make a steady income so I can show the court I am stable enough to be awarded custody of my sister.

Thoughts of becoming a parent instead of enjoying my college experience dampen my mood. Since I don't plan on getting married or pregnant anytime soon, maybe I will become a foster parent or adopt a child in need. I refuse to bring a child into this harsh world. No matter what, I will ensure I can provide an unwavering foundation of love and support. I want to save a child's life and not just my sister's. I want to offer them the nurturing embrace and the unconditional love their hearts desperately seek.

Why do I even get down on myself, knowing I have parented her most of our lives? Maybe that is where all this built-up anger comes from—when I should have been enjoying my childhood, I was taking care of my mother's daughter. The foster care system did what it could. I can't be ungrateful, but that same system could have done better verifying the foster parents. If they had checked the information, they would have recognized the fraudulent education documentation, which would have ultimately disqualified them from ever having the opportunity to abuse Nicole and me.

The rule from the foster care agency was "no physical discipline." Catarina knew what she was doing. Even Santiago, three times Nicole's slender teenage size, dismissed that rule when he physically chased my sister around the dining room table to swat her with his thick leather belt.

But what can I do? She is there, and I am here. My only hope is to keep moving forward.

CHAPTER 14

Ten years ago.

Today, Santi and Catarina sign the paperwork to take custody of the girls. She doesn't consider them their daughters—just *the girls*. They are not cute enough to be considered Catarina's kids. They walk into the building, and the smell of pumpkin spice floods her nostrils. She loves this time of the year.

This is the season she collects a variety of stories to share with church members, encouraging them to make generous donations. This year, she'll make it easy by spreading the word about the girls and embellishing their circumstances. That should inspire people to lend a helping hand.

People are always so charitable during the holidays. She looks forward to the cash, clothes, and gifts to accompany the government benefits, food assistance, transportation, and housing assistance checks. The agency even offers vouchers to set up these orphans!

Catarina's reward for keeping these girls alive is substantial. She can sell her car now. After all, they are providing her with transportation funds to cover a reliable vehicle ensuring the orphans make it to their appointments and school. She won't have to continue looking for a job because they cover five hundred dollars a month per child in food and grocery expenses. As the wheels turn in her head, Catarina calculates the coming tsunami of extra income. *I don't understand why there are so many of them in the system if getting them kids makes money so easily!*

"Please sign here and here." The lady at the desk points to the X on the paper in front of her.

They sign the documents and listen to the lady ramble about no drugs, no alcohol, no spanking, no physical discipline of any sort. The lady refuses to shut up, and Catarina refrains from rolling her eyes. *She is as dumb as my left toe if she thinks I won't whoop the crap out of Gina's kids! After all, Gina owes me a few.*

She remembers the party she took Gina to when those old men were so friendly with her. She was lucky Catarina told them to cut it short. If she had been so mean, as Gina said, she would have let it go on longer than the thirty minutes they paid for. Gina wanted to tell the whole town they took advantage of her, but her mom didn't believe her.

Catarina didn't even feel bad when she found out Gina's mom beat her after she shared about the assault. Maybe she should have charged the men more to have their way. Catarina made one hundred dollars to set up her best friend. All she had to do was invite Gina to the party, tell her she didn't want to go to the bathroom alone, then lock her inside. Gina was so tiny, it was easy to get out of the bathroom without her putting up a fight. *The dumb girl always trusted me.*

At the sound of a security door buzzing open, Catarina looks up. The girls ease past the guard. They are so skinny. Prominent cheekbones make her question whether they have eaten in months. It looks like these two girls are addicts, like their mother. They are practically skin and bones! She needs to fatten them up because she will not have people thinking she starves anyone!!

A fake smile forces its way out to greet them. Santi is much nicer because he leans in for a hug to welcome them into their family. These kids look homeless. From their bony appearance to their matted hair, the apple sure doesn't fall far from the tree.

They walk to their meager form of transportation. The girls wait for direction, bothering Catarina already. She spent several years training her own girls along with her husband, so they already know what needs to be done without her instruction. They shouldn't have to be told what to do! It is common sense to open the door, get into the car, and buckle up their seat belts. But these girls are standing outside with confused expressions, as if they aren't sure of the next move. My kids are so much brighter.

Catarina doesn't call the little girls out on their stupidity. Letting it slide, she opens the back passenger door and hurries the girls inside the car. She maintains her forced smile as she guides them just in case the cameras outside the agency building work. The girls are shy and quiet throughout the drive to the mobile home park. Santi takes his focus from the ongoing traffic and taps his elbow against Catarina's left arm, recommending she welcome the girls, too.

"We should try to be nice to them. You never know." He pauses for a second and lowers his voice. "It might work out better for us."

He adjusts his driving position and uses his brakes to come to a complete stop, allowing the pedestrian on the sidewalk to cross the street. Catarina wants to explode at the man's kindness, but she must remain calm. Staying calm is all part of the plan.

Until they finalize the process, she must treat their new foster daughters as nicely as possible. She will manipulate them just enough to believe she genuinely cares about them. *Deep down, I couldn't care less what happens to them. Their own mother doesn't give a....* Someone honks to urge Santi forward into the intersection.

Catarina doesn't believe anyone should have to carry that burden. Her animosity is not just toward Gina. If addicts don't tend to their kids, why should anyone else? She is doing this for a check—not because she cares. They're her meal ticket for the next decade.

For most of the evening, Catarina browses the web, researching different minivan models. Since the foster agency covers the cost of a new vehicle, she plans to take full advantage and will choose the most expensive one at the dealership. Completely paid off vehicle with no monthly payment! If she was not the one living it, she would for sure think this is a scam.

Catarina reaches over to the coffee table and grabs her ringing cell phone. The caller ID shows it is her sister. *I wonder what Yazzy wants at this time of night.* Yazzy, short for Yazmin, has been her older sister's nickname since childhood.

"Hi, Yazzy. Long time."

"Hi. Hello, Catarina. How is it going with your new daughters?"

Disgust fills Catarina's voice as she silences her sister's cheerful tone.

"Daughters?"

"No offense, Catarina, but did you and Santiago not sign up as foster parents for your friend's girls?"

"First, Yazzy, those girls aren't my daughters. Second, yes, we did, and thank you for asking. But never compare these orphans to my own blood!" Catarina looks down at her screen to see if her sister hung up, but she is still on the line.

"So, are you gonna say anything or not, Yazmin? I don't have time for this."

Her sister's voice quivers audibly, and it angers Catarina to know Yazzy is her polar opposite with kids. Tenderhearted Yazzy would never dream of hurting a fly, much less a child. Sisterhood implies shared confidence, but not these sisters. Catarina hides things. If Yazzy discovers who she is, she would want nothing to do with her. No matter Catarina's situation, she is an opportunist—and this is the perfect opportunity.

Aside from her husband and kids, she does not have anyone other than Yazmin and her brother-in-law, Reggie. Their mother occasionally calls her, but if Catarina doesn't reach out, then she won't hear from her.

After the divorce from Dwayne, her mother slowly distanced herself from Santiago and Catarina. She claimed their act of fornication inside the church was quite an embarrassment. *As religious as she is, I don't think she has forgiven me. She probably never will. I doubt I would forgive my daughter, Celi, if she had done what I did at her age.*

Introducing Annie and Nicole to her kids is easy. They seem to get along fine, even though they have an age gap. Unlike Catarina's daughters, the orphan girls remain silent and instantly obey. Celi and Jen are snobs. As their mother, she knows exactly who her daughters are.

Her youngest baby, Celi, is her precious angel. But her oldest daughter, Jen, hates her. She is working on that, though. Catarina can't manipulate her with words because Jen has no problem calling her out. She also has no filter, so whatever she is thinking escapes her mouth. Jen knows Catarina is always working some angle. Her oldest daughter is only here to meet Annie and Nicole. She doesn't live with them during the week, choosing instead to stay with her dad and his live-in girlfriend.

Trying to destroy Dwayne's current girlfriend's life did not turn out well for Catarina. She learned the hard way, too. The girlfriend's front doorbell camera caught Catarina on video keying her brand-new car. She had a field day sharing footage of her new boyfriend's ex dragging a flathead screwdriver from one end of her car to the other. There was not enough damage from Catarina's point of view, so she emptied a can of expired sardines under the hood. Had the camera not caught it, she would have gone days or weeks wondering where the stench was coming from.

Catarina did not know the girl's name for months. Then, when she finally got her name out of Jen, she could not understand why they were trying so hard to keep her from finding out. She was a broke nobody who barely had an education—nothing special to her.

Still, she didn't give in to Catarina's games or any other attempts at agitation. Catarina ended up just getting angry with herself for not being able to affect the other woman and eventually stopped. Nobody told her to leave her alone. She didn't feel the desire to bother her anymore. Every time she tried to text her, calling her names, insulting her, or cursing her out, she never failed to respond the same way.

"Catarina, I do pray for your broken heart. I forgive you for trying to destroy me. But don't you get it? I am covered with the blood of Jesus!" Her words always give Catarina chills to think about, and not once did that woman ever put up a fight.

Who cares whether she is good for Dwayne? She is different, and she is good to Jen. Nothing else really matters.

The sight of her girls and the other kids hitting it off catches Catarina's eye across the room. *I don't know who those girls think they are, but they are already getting too comfortable.* Her rumbling stomach has her yearning for the corner convenience store that sells ready-to-eat cheeseburgers for ninety-nine cents. They haven't raised the price in a decade.

She expects both girls to say they are not hungry since she already fed them a bowl of cereal this morning. Catarina doesn't cook breakfast for her own kids, much less someone else's. Plus, she hates the smell of scrambled eggs. They make the house smell disgusting. Eggs are for cake mix—nothing else.

Catarina heads out to grab the cheeseburgers, but she'll eat them before she returns home. *Sorry girls, they ran out.*

CHAPTER 15

Present Day

Since we ended the call, the conversation with Nicole has me feeling uneasy. We talked about her birthday coming up, an unexpected gift from their foster mother, and how I might visit her if I can catch a ride from a friend. We didn't chat very long, but I find it odd Catarina would get Nicole a new bike. I lived with that woman long enough to know she does nothing from the kindness of her heart—I don't think she has one!

An urge to call Catarina overwhelms me. I want to threaten her—tell her the games have to stop unless she wants me to report her to the authorities again. As much as I want to do that, I can't. I hold myself back because I know better than anyone else if I so much as breathe incorrectly during our conversation, she will make my sister pay for it.

I kick the throw pillow across the floor. Staring at my phone, I search for answers to questions I cannot ask.

I type into the search bar: *Is it normal for your parents to say and do mean things to you?* I skim over the very first paragraph that pops up with an answer. Apparently, it is not normal, and there is a number urging victims to call if they are experiencing mental or verbal abuse.

I fill the rest of my day browsing the web and learning about different types of abuse—most of which I am surprised to learn I have experienced firsthand. My roommate interrupts my browsing with a road trip invitation. I haven't been on many trips, but it sounds like a much-needed vacation.

"Come on!! You have to tag along, pleeease!!" She tugs at my arm while whining like a toddler. "You will get to meet my mom, too! She's cool!"

It's technically a girl's trip, because Mitsy also invited the girls across the hallway to join us. She is such a people person.

Without further explanation, Mitsy, Imani-Rain, Eunique, and I crowd inside Mitsy's Honda CRV. The SUV has no air conditioning in the triple-digit heat, and we wedge in like sardines. These girls have no concept of packing light. I can't afford to lose the only friends I have made this semester, so I keep my thoughts to myself. It's what I am good at.

Being honest with Catarina was impossible when she asked my opinion. She inquired an abnormal number of times what those around her were thinking—myself included—another need to control everything.

Mitsy mentions her mom will meet us there, but I loathe the thought of it. I have never met her mother, so my intense feelings about her are weird.

Some secrets I keep close. I rarely envy girls who are prettier than me, possess a more attractive body than mine, or even effortlessly capture the attention of any guy in the room. I don't even have jealous feelings toward the girls who are smarter than me and excel academically beyond my abilities. However, seeing someone share a nurturing relationship with their parents stirs those feelings of jealousy every time.

It doesn't matter to me if those children describe their parents as flawed or dysfunctional. The simple fact they have parents who choose to be part of their lives feels like grace I will never receive. Having parents who affirm your existence and support and care for you is an invaluable treasure—an absolute blessing.

Social media is indeed the thief of joy. Comparing my life of survival without parents to a fortunate kid with the gift of sharing love with their parents fills me with profound longing. Honestly, kids with parents who choose them are undoubtedly the luckiest human beings.

Reading an incoming message from Nicole makes my heart sink. I just told her I would make a trip to see her on her birthday, and here I am, making plans to hit the road with my new friends. I failed to keep my word, and the guilt kicks in.

Between balancing work, going to school, and looking for internships, I forgot about Nicole's birthday. I thought Catarina had some evil motive behind gifting Nicole a new bike, but maybe it was a birthday gift. For once, I hope there are no evil motives behind her acts. Catarina got my sister a birthday gift? Maybe she has changed.

The glimpse of hope comes from my daily prayers. I pray every day God renews Catarina's heart. My hope comes from God alone.

So far, the trip is pleasant. Surprisingly, Mitsy's mom is pretty cool. I feel different about this mother-daughter duo because their relationship seems more like they're friends. Mitsy's mom does not dress like your average mother either. She even introduced herself as "Misty's fab mom."

It has been well over twenty-four hours, and I still haven't asked her name. I met the lady with her "girls" out, exposing cleavage from a shirt that looks like she grabbed it from the children's section and a skin-tight leather skirt barely covering anything. Mitsy's mom comes into the sitting room where we are all hanging out and wants to know the plans for the night.

"I was thinking we could enjoy this cabin and watch scary movies." Imani-Rain is a horror movie connoisseur.

"How about no!" Eunique points her index finger. "I vote we go to the casino!"

There is no way they will let me inside a casino. I'm probably not the only one who's too young, but most of them have fake IDs. Still, we came to enjoy the trip, not get arrested.

"Pretty sure the casino is off limits for me."

"Did y'all know I got bribed to go to college?" Mitsy catches my drift and changes the subject. She's always got my back.

Imani-Rain raises her eyebrows in astonishment at Mitsy's random question. The atmosphere thickens as her mother's expression shifts from surprise to annoyance. With a sharp twist of her neck, she glares at Mitsy, her voice rising with noticeable frustration.

"Oh, shut it, Mitsy! I didn't bribe you. I offered you a little something to spark your motivation so you don't end up like me—relying on men to pay the bills!" Mitsy's cheeks turn bright pink, and her eyes roll dramatically.

My roommate's exasperation bewilders me. I can't fathom why she would resist her mother's words of caution. All I know is if I ever rolled my eyes like that in front of Catarina, she would have smacked them into my brain!

A part of me longs for a glimpse of parental wisdom—a desire for guidance from the people who brought me into this world. If only my parents had been there to offer me advice or share a memory. Maybe I would have understood the weight of my traumatic upbringing.

Parents typically bear wisdom and knowledge from their harsh lives and the challenges they've faced. Most parents do their best to keep their children from making the same mistakes. Unfortunately, I never had parents—not really. I guess I'll just have to make my own mistakes without them.

From a young age, I have questioned why we were not enough for our mother to devote her life to selflessly raising us. While it's simple to enumerate the failures of a lousy mother, of which both my foster mother and birth-giver certainly provide a vivid example, I find my thoughts drifting to my own aspirations. I used to believe I had no heroes—only reflections of what I didn't want to become. They fueled my ambition to succeed. The idea I am the hero of my story feels mentally exhausting. I give it some thought today as we arrive back on campus.

While strolling through the grounds, the dandelions instantly remind me of my true hero. They are strong and persevere in the harshest of conditions. I am not designed to be the hero of my story.

My admiration swells for the woman who gave everything to end up with nothing. Sometimes, they work over forty hours a week just to have enough to put food on the table. And they rarely wear capes. Sometimes, heroes are the grandmothers trying to raise their grandchildren.

Chapter 16

My mother's given name is Gina. I noticed her problem at an early age. The extent remained unclear, yet I felt the unease. She would drop Nicole and me off at a local department store—one of those 24/7 places with doors that never locked. Nicole still drank from a bottle. We were both too young for school.

In the beginning, she dropped us at the store in the mornings, promising to return shortly, but eventually, I knew the drill. Gina would drop us off, lock us inside the private dressing room, and return after several hours—sometimes days.

I made a promise to always look out for Nicole, no matter what. I vowed to take care of her myself because I understood the opposite. Not knowing why left me feeling despondent. Absent feelings of love and care from my parents played an astronomical role in my childhood trauma. It was not a physical cry for them to want me—it was an internal scream begging for their love.

I longed for their devotion my entire life, yet they chose every reason to refrain from it. My mother chose drugs. My father chose everything but fatherhood. Surely, they took one look at both of their daughters and decided we weren't enough for them to continue walking out the path of parental responsibility. Given the passage of time, it seems only logical. Not knowing the answer to my parent's absence left me full of questions.

I faked life for so long I lost track of the moment it all began. Somewhere along the way, I drifted from my limits, identity, and even sense of self-worth. I felt overwhelming anger toward the world, channeling my frustration into blaming my past traumas, which seemed more straightforward than delving into the complexities of my own emotions and experiences.

In truth, I never held onto grand dreams like others my age. My greatest desire is a safe, welcoming home. This isn't a plea for sympathy. The privilege of nurturing big dreams feels unattainable. Those of us from broken homes simply hope for stability, longing for the day we can let down our guard and just be.

I used to feel like a burden to those around me until I realized I needed to prioritize myself. At that exact moment, I decided I would no longer feel sorry for my situation. I refuse to be another statistic as a victim of my own circumstances. I will not allow it—especially if I hope to save Nicole.

Chapter 17

Unpacking after a trip is on my list of least favorite things to do. I have met no one who genuinely enjoys unpacking. Every time, my suitcase full of wrinkled clothes whispers from its new home at the base of my bed, berating me for ignoring it.

My mornings are a blur of activity, especially Mondays. I wake up early, grab a bite, and rush to class. Even when I feel sick, I attend class. I can't afford to miss a day of lectures and fall behind. After class, I dash across campus to clock in for my shift at the nearby cafe, feeling exhausted before the day has truly begun.

Today is different. I wake up feeling incredibly sick, waves of nausea washing over me, making it impossible to focus on anything but how miserable I feel. Starting the week like this is a challenge—how will I handle my responsibilities? I depend on every penny I earn from my paycheck, so calling into work today feels like a significant risk.

I spend most of the morning hugging the cool rim of porcelain, expelling the contents of my stomach. My body aches from the constant tug of war between sweating and shivering. Whatever causes this misery, the sensation is awful.

When I finally call my manager to report my absence, a curt response greets me. He seems dismissive, but maybe there's some kind of stomach bug making its way around.

"You and the rest of the world."

As I reach for my phone from the pile of tissues on the bathroom sink, I notice several missed calls from an unknown number. I don't stress much over numbers I don't recognize, but seeing four missed calls feels excessive. It seems unlikely someone would dial the wrong number multiple times without realizing their mistake.

My curiosity piqued, I hit the redial button. To my shock, the call connects to a county jail facility. Confusion washes over me, so I disconnect without a word.

"You good?" Mitsy's voice sounds concerned as she eyes me across the room.

"Yeah, someone just tried to call from a jail."

Mitsy leaps out of her seat and positions herself right in front of me, her eyes wide with curiosity and face twisted in confusion.

"Are you into that kind of thing?"

For about two minutes, Mitsy expounds on a show she watched about people willingly dating inmates. She shares intriguing tidbits about these individuals who send money and care packages to inmates they've never met, even forming deep emotional connections leading to marriage. As she continues to talk to me about inmates and jail, I try to listen to her foreign banter. When I can't contain my thoughts any longer, I interrupt.

"Mitsy, not today!"

I usually take pride in being a good listener, but today, I struggle with her stories. Her high-pitched voice seems to pierce the early morning air, and it overstimulates me—it's 7 AM and I'm sick!

Mitsy and I are opposites. If someone were to make a comment like that to me, I would probably retreat into a depressive state and cry. But Mitsy? She brushes off my frigid response with a dismissive wave and walks away. Though Mitsy seems unaffected by my outburst, I am surprised she didn't ask if I was okay. She has a habit of checking in on my well-being.

Mitsy gives me space for the remainder of our day, diverting her attention to whatever activities fill her hours when she's not in class or in the dorm room. I imagine her heading out with friends of her choice—vibrant and social—while I sit here alone with my thoughts, a lingering sense of discomfort.

There is a high possibility we would not be friends if dorm room assignments had not forced Mitsy and me together. Although we share similar interests and struggles, she is not the typical girl I voluntarily approach for friendship. Certain women naturally exude popularity. I find it disconcerting. Ironically, my roommate is growing on me. The more I get to know Mitsy, the more I learn to love her quirks.

I hear buzzing from my phone, and the vibration reminds me I silenced my ringer. I muster the strength to lift my frail body into a sitting position and begin searching for the device. What a day today has been.

My dorm room, shy of 250 square feet, becomes a mansion as I struggle to navigate the clutter while my head swims. This game of hide-and-seek with my phone is annoying me. Oops! There it is. I spot the lights flashing as the vibrating continues. My fingertips brush against the cold screen as I snatch it from between my used calculus textbook and a black three-ring binder. Without glancing at the caller ID, I answer.

Who could be calling me from jail? Familiar tension creeps up my spine, matching the charge of the surrounding air. I punch in my credit card number. I'm not just the recipient of this collect call—I'm also paying the bill. This unsettling lesson is unimaginable at my age. When someone in jail reaches out, the person outside pays for the fleeting connection.

"Goodness, Nicole, why are you in jail?! Is this some sort of prank you want to pull on me? Tell me what happened NOW! Nicole, I am serious! What happened?!"

My mind jumbles with anger and confusion, and the air thickens with unsettling anticipation. My short interrogation must have Nicole thinking. Her sudden breakdown pierces the silence, a haunting melody that reverberates in my mind. I cannot see the tears behind the echo of pain I've only heard once before from my baby sister. That unwanted sound lives in my head.

The day we parted from Grandma Sally marked our entry into the unfamiliar world of foster care. It all stemmed from my recklessness, a desperate attempt, a decision influenced by Catarina—my mother's best friend. As a child, I foolishly listened to her and unknowingly sealed our fate. At not even eight years old, I fell for her deceit and manipulation.

I should have never listened to Catarina's threats, because maybe Nicole and I would have been better off staying with our grandma. I was too young to understand what Catarina was doing. They removed us solely because of my grandmother's neglect of not seeking help after the sexual abuse. Except, my grandma didn't know. Catarina was the only person I told because she was my mom's best friend!

"Was your grandma aware of the sexual abuse and still failed to take you to get medically examined?" Eyes wide, I nodded my head at the questioning officer. After hearing Catarina say they would take me away for not telling the cops my grandma knew, I panicked. I trusted her. I don't know why, but I did. She promised me Nicole's safety—and Disneyland!

If only I held my ground against Catarina's scheming or summoned the courage to resist her conniving grasp, perhaps we could have avoided all of this. That woman is a master manipulator! As I listen to Nicole weep, I can feel my shoulders burdened with the weight crashing down on both of us.

"I didn't want to do it. You know how she is. I just did it because she told me!" Nicole's voice trembles as the realization of Catarina's influence hits me hard—she has finally twisted my sister's innocence into something dark. Catarina has Nicole believing the lies that led her into this trap. She turned an innocent little girl into a pawn in a criminal's dangerous game.

The reality grows more transparent with each passing moment. Catarina has already found her next victim. Now that I'm out of the picture, my innocent sister gets the short end of the stick. Nicole recounts the events leading up to this moment, including several prior arrests for petty theft at Catarina's coercion. Their foster mother spent the money meant for rent and then compelled her to steal once again from Ms. Corrine.

For a moment, I am relieved to hear a neighbor caught Catarina around the area during the break-in at Mrs. Corrine's. But the relief quickly morphs into dread as Nicole shares the neighbor's poor eyesight kept her from identifying Catarina when it mattered. Just like that, the perpetrator is Nicole—a teenager who now carries the burden of a felony charge because Mrs. Corrine's jewelry wasn't the cheap stuff.

I need an attorney to help my sister. What lies ahead for her if I don't untangle Catarina's web of deceit? I can't continue to allow Nicole to live with a criminal mastermind. Only a treacherous path lies ahead. I brace myself for the inevitable whirlwind of turmoil.

Our phone call cuts off without a proper goodbye. I have no familiarity with jail regulations, but they should allow more than five minutes on a phone call. After all, I am the one paying for it!

An icy hand of uncertainty tightens its grip on my heart.

Chapter 18

This weekend, I refuse to take part in the vibrant campus activities, including a spirited pep rally and colorful parades that excite the student body. Instead, I focus on finding legal support for Nicole. Staying with her in that environment—with Catarina—would have slimmed our chances of escape to none. The weight of my baby sister's situation is palpable. Catarina did not hold us hostage. I am sure if we wanted to leave, we could. She just made the options difficult! Where do you go when you're a teenager? I knew what would happen to us if I told someone about it. I quickly learned leaving was an invitation for violence.

There were plenty of times I ran away. I was probably eleven or twelve the first time. I slept in a public park inside a plastic tunnel slide. Thank God it was mid-July, and the summer nights were in the high 70s. Catarina reported me missing to protect herself, then acted accordingly. She cried, twisted the narrative, made people feel sorry for her, and got whatever she wanted—the blame always fell on the "troubled" child.

The cop who spotted me at the park approached me, asking why I was not in school. He heard me out, then directed me toward his patrol car. At first, I felt scared, thinking he was arresting me, but he was nice. He took me back to Catarina's house, where I faced severe consequences for my actions.

She hit me, even when I did nothing wrong. I remember cheerfully singing along to a Justin Bieber song one time when her bare hand connected with my face. Since I am still unsure what prompted the slap, my singing voice is now a barely audible whisper.

Another time, I ran away and made it out of state—before we moved to San Diego. I walked and walked and walked. After ninety miles on foot, I made it to my aunt's house, hoping for rescue. Instead, I found myself dropped at a homeless shelter. She called the police, rejecting the responsibility of my care. Blood might make her my aunt, but her actions revealed what we truly mean to each other—*nothing*. She discarded me at her earliest convenience, just like my mother.

The volunteer lady at the shelter was so kind as she helped me throughout my stay. It's been such a long time I can't remember her name, but the look of astonishment on her face while talking to Catarina lives engraved on my brain. Catarina's response shocked her when she let her know the situation and my need for a ride home. Shutting down the offer with her hasty response, Catarina informed her she was not driving almost one hundred miles away to pick up a "bad kid" who needed to learn her lesson. The volunteer's tight hug and raspy whisper imprinted on my core.

"That's not a mother. No mother who cares for their child would ever say such a thing. You deserve to be loved, young lady! Go big, and don't let someone cruel like her get the best of you."

She kindly allowed me to reach out to someone else for help, but when I shared there was no one I could call, she offered to contact a case worker who might find someone from my biological family to come for me. Thankfully, this led to locating the brother I had never met and his wife.

My long-lost brother, Dallas, and his wife, Tiffany, drove to pick me up from the shelter—rescuing me without hesitation. To this day, they mean the absolute world to me. I had always heard rumors in my family about an older brother whom none of us had met, not even my grandma. My mother gave birth and promptly left him with his dad. Never fed him, never changed a diaper for this baby, nothing. Just left him. He grew up doing better for himself. They lived several hours away from the shelter, but I will never forget how welcoming they were during those few months I stayed with them.

Unfortunately, Catarina interrupted those happy times when she showed up unannounced and unwelcome at their door. Tiffany stood her ground with the courage that only comes from a mother trying to protect her babies. Her exact words echo in my mind, vivid and unforgettable. "No way, Catarina! If you step one more foot on my property, I'll pick up a charge!"

The sheer intensity of her declaration sent shock waves through the air, and I would pay top dollar to witness the look of disbelief on Catarina's face again as she absorbed the harsh truth. Her complexion drained of color, and her jaw dropped.

Tiffany defended her sanctuary—the home where she nurtured her family—with a fierce resolve every mother should embrace. She was prepared to protect her loved ones from all perceived threats by any means necessary. I felt like one of Tiffany's children that day. Witnessing someone confront Catarina Coyazo with fearless defiance to protect me overwhelms me still!

Even as Catarina attempted to twist the narrative, lying through her teeth about my so-called misdeeds and how I had become uncontrollable, Tiffany stood her ground. My aching mind and frail body were living testaments to the struggles I faced, starkly contrasting Catarina's distorted portrayal. Under Tiffany's passionate shelter, I felt a glimmer of hope and safety—one I had never known before.

Unfortunately, Catarina had a knack for staying in the good graces of those who could help her gain whatever her heart desired. Child Services protected her rights as a foster mother and ensured the police took me back to California. I despise the memory of this person who willingly became a foster parent, only to offer me a relationship with a hefty price tag.

Once I returned to Catarina's home, her expectations of me increased. Nicole and I were her piggy banks—they won't make you rich overnight, but they're good to have around. It was only a matter of time before the petty thefts caught up to us.

Spotting my laptop, I log on to search for information on what to do if you suspect someone is being forced to commit crimes. I dive deep into a rabbit hole, one of which consumes the rest of my day.

Chapter 19

After today's classes and my evening shift at work, I will use every penny I've painstakingly saved from my paychecks to hire an affordable, skilled criminal defense attorney for Nicole. I am prepared to take out multiple loans, no matter the cost, to ensure she doesn't take the fall for something she would have never done voluntarily.

Nicole hasn't called me in two days, and the silence unnerves me. Mitsy has been away all weekend, and I miss her bubbly personality more than expected. I am the friend who thrives on hugs and warmth, while Mitsy prefers to keep her distance—a trait she shares with Nicole.

Everywhere I turn lately, I see reminders of my baby sister. The bright petals on flowers blooming throughout campus. reflect her cheerful laughter and kindness. My subconscious tugs at my brain to keep her at the forefront of my thoughts. I feel helpless about Nicole's situation.

An unsettling feeling of anger forms in the pit of my stomach. As her big sister, I took responsibility to care for her, even at the expense of my own well-being. As an adult, I should have more rights to help Nicole, but a college kid with no home or disposable income can only do so much. I am determined to fight and explore every avenue to help my sister.

After reaching out multiple times and leaving numerous voicemails, I finally return a call from an attorney who graciously left a voicemail to schedule a consultation with her firm. The moment she answers, her aggressive tone strikes me—she sounds like a bully. Perhaps it's my inability to pick up on her intended message, but I can't shake off that first impression.

A bill featuring Benjamin Franklin for this 30-minute phone call might be overkill, but to me, it's the equivalent of several months of intense research. During the first few minutes of our consultation, the attorney expresses her concern regarding Nicole's case and outlines her predictions for what might happen if I proceed without proper defense.

The law firm's website features a professional headshot of an older woman with a full head of silver tresses. She seems classy, and her gray locks convince me she has extensive experience in this field. Despite never meeting her in person, I trust her. Her voice carries a hint of southern twang, uncommon in this area. She is not a local.

The consultation feels rushed and overwhelming, but she instills a glimmer of hope in me. The attorney suggests if I hire her, they can save Nicole from going to a federal prison. However, one critical issue looms over us. Nicole may be a minor, but the state has charged her as an adult. This is only possible in serious crime cases. It's almost surreal.

Catarina Coyazo, our lovely foster mother, diverted the entire narrative, placing all the blame squarely on Nicole's shoulders. Lacking cameras or witnesses to corroborate the events, except for an unreliable elderly neighbor, it is as Catarina always predicted—her word against a "troubled" foster kid.

She always twists the truth to position herself as the victim while casting everyone else in a negative light. Astonishingly, a person as evil as Catarina can manipulate the system with ease to portray an innocent teenager as the mastermind of a felony-level crime. Although it's a sad reality, the criminal has outsmarted justice. How is it possible for someone so deceitful to evade the consequences of their actions for such a long time?

Though the attorney's consultation sounds promising, I need to delve deeper into whether she is worth the expense. My professor is a retired attorney.

Perhaps he can recommend someone reliable who won't just sell me false hope.

The anger surging within me demands an outlet. Before I fully process my decision, my fingers dial Catarina's number. Her name brings up a flood of emotions, but she rejects my call. What a coward! Certainly she suspects the reason for my call. I need to unleash my pent-up frustration.

It's easier for her to press the red button than to face the consequences of her actions. Reflecting on all my sister and I have endured from this toxic family infuriates me. All our hopes of feeling loved and accepted as their own were nothing more than pipe dreams. What kind of person would even consider coercing a child into doing something illegal? Catarina Coyazo, that's who. She embodies a cruelty that's unfathomable.

My endless day drags on, and I want to indulge in some greasy fast food. Honestly, I prefer real comfort food, but it dances in a distant dream I can't quite access without a second job. Right now, frugality must take priority to stretch every penny until I can hire an attorney to represent Nicole.

I absolutely love Nicole. She is not only my baby sister. She's a piece of my heart. Without her, a chunk of my existence would die. Now, more than ever, the weight of our struggles crushes me—an invisible mass

I can't seem to avoid. I envision the day I can afford to buy a cozy home for both of us, a place where we can feel safe and secure under our own names—an unshakable foundation nobody can take from us.

Every day, the desire to give Nicole a better life fuels my motivation to earn my degree. I am desperate for things to improve for us both. We've endured so much together, and it burdens my heart to think of Nicole as scared and alone. The haunting silence since our last phone call increases with my understanding of Nicole's problematic position. I hate to admit it, but she had no choice but to comply. That woman controls everyone around her.

I will never forgive myself if something happens to Nicole. She deserves so much more than what life has thrown our way. I cannot bear to lose my connection with Nicole because of circumstances beyond our control. This burden overwhelms me. Having parents sure would be nice right about now. I yearn for a simplified existence for both of us, and I worry about the reason Nicole has not called me again.

The repercussions are worse if she resists compliance with Catarina's demands. Clearly aware of Catarina's manipulative, controlling capabilities, I note the gravity of the situation. Nicole's prospects for a viable future are exceedingly bleak without my intervention. If I do not help her, nobody else will.

The obligation to help Nicole burdens my conscience. I cannot bear the thought of Catarina hurting her anymore.

Tomorrow, I have two more midterm exams on my schedule. But when I finish my evening shift, if it is not too late, I plan to call that attorney and hire her to represent Nicole.

Chapter 20

Before she discovered Annie's college intentions, Catarina assumed she would take the fall for her like she always did. But that isn't what happened.

About a month before she left, while trying to pawn a stolen ring, Annie refused orders. She actually said the word No. With her big mouth and beaver teeth sticking out, she said she would no longer be Catarina's puppet. There were other words escaping her trap, but her foster mother wouldn't hear them, even with her freedom on the line. "No" was more than Catarina could handle. No one told Catarina Coyazo, "No!" No one.

"Oh, you have no idea what you're doing, you little brat! It's game on, like Donkey Kong." Neither of them had a clue what that meant, but it's what Catarina told Annie, anyway. And the threat behind it was real.

Catarina always liked a challenge, especially when the game relieved her frustrations. Every day after that, she told herself Annie would pay for the choice to disobey. *She needs to learn how to respect me, and if*

I tell her to jump, she better ask me how freaking high. No, Catarina didn't feel an ounce of remorse.

Would a simple "thank you" from either of them hurt? They should thank her for opening her home to them. After all, if she hadn't proceeded with her plan to get custody, they would have separated the girls forever.

Annie was a tidy girl. She never thanked Catarina for such quality training, either. Anytime those girls showed signs of boredom, she had them cleaning the walls from ceiling to floor, corner to corner. She loves a clean home but hates to clean.

That was never a problem, though. At the snap of her fingers, Annie and Nicole would run to obey her commands—RUN!. From her recliner, she would bellow her angry demands at Annie and Nicole just to watch their terrified expressions. Thinking of it now draws wicked laughter from Catarina's throat.

Her thoughts focus on the older of the two orphan girls. *She will need me much quicker than I'll ever need her. I think of her, but I don't miss her. I miss my slave, not the orphan. Mainly because of that mouth of hers!* Annie always tried to get smart with Catarina, asking stupid questions.

"Do you ever feel bad about how you treat us?" The miserable girl's eyes brimmed with tears as the accusatory question flew from her lips.

"Absolutely not! If you had a mother who actually cared about you, maybe I would think twice."

No sane person would ever put themselves in a position to face an angry mother, after all. *If anyone ever treated my girls the way I have Annie and Nicole, believe me, I'd be on death row!* They don't have anyone who cares, though. No one will come to their rescue, so no one will stop Catarina from treating them exactly as she desires.

Annie repeatedly tried and failed to report her foster mother to the state agency. She probably thought she got away with it, but when Catarina found out the girl was going to college, she decided to enact her revenge. It was a slam dunk. Nicole would have no choice but to stay behind. Annie couldn't afford to take her sister, too. And everyone knows the easiest way to get to Annie is to use Nicole as bait.

Nicole is a good kid—this might not be as enjoyable as Catarina hoped. The younger orphan doesn't have much of a big mouth. She is quiet, very quiet, and never asks questions like her sister. Annie always asked question after question—so annoying. No wonder Catarina swatted her face so much. Annie even tried to open her big mouth and tell the caseworker about the clothing vouchers. That girl doesn't have a clue! She should have never left Nicole alone. She should have ridden it out here until Nicole was old enough to go, too. But she'll learn.

Annie always tackled the hard tasks. Perhaps Nicole possesses similar capabilities. Annie was a five-finger discount pro at the stores. Then, Catarina would have her post them on the local online buy and sell pages. Baby clothing was the easiest to move. Plus, it made exceptional gifts for Jen—whenever she actually came around to visit with her kid.

Catarina would go inside the store, put everything she wanted into the shopping cart, and have Annie run out with the entire basket. She would tell her to run and keep running until she found their truck. Catarina chuckles now at the image of Annie's skinny legs running with the grocery basket at full speed, careful to prevent anything from falling. Annie knew better than to let a single item touch the ground.

That girl never thanked Catarina for her smarts, either! She noticed it when Annie suggested picking up receipts from the ground, going into the store to get everything listed on the paid receipt, pretending to check out in the self-pay line, and then walking right out the front door. The idea baffled Catarina. *I didn't need her for diddly-squat anymore.*

Catarina was whatever she could be to them. There must have been a reason nobody took them in. When they wanted to separate them, she stepped up to the plate to do another woman's job and kept those girls together. She gave them a roof over their head and fed them. There were a few times Santi had to discipline Nicole with his leather belt. But only a few, because she quickly learned not to test him. Annie, though—that girl was a walking headache. She was never grateful for anything.

Now, revenge for her ungrateful disobedience begins. Annie will pay for Gina's mistakes. Nicole will pay for Annie's. Their pleas for love fall on deaf ears. Everyone will pay.

Chapter 21

The phone trills as Annie's name flashes on the screen. *What does that parasite want? She already cost me half a paycheck every month because she graduated early.* But Catarina knows exactly why she is calling. She wants to complain about Nicole being in jail. Well, that's just too bad. Catarina thrusts her finger against the red button on her screen. Annie is no longer her responsibility. She didn't want her, anyway.

The moment they stopped sending checks for that girl was the moment Catarina told Santi *the parasite* had to go. They waited exactly twenty-four hours after Annie's high school graduation to cut off her support. Had Catarina known that was going to happen, she would have never allowed an early graduation. But it never crossed her mind. *Annie is remarkably clever. She's even brighter than I am.* Catarina fights to acknowledge a drug addict's child might exhibit superior intelligence.

Instead, she calls the phone company to report Annie's phone stolen in retaliation for her intellect. They shut off service to the phone and will tell her the location when it turns on again. Catarina takes it a step further, instructing the phone company to alert law enforcement regarding the theft. It is a newer iPhone, priced over a thousand dollars. If they catch her, wherever she is, she will face a felony charge, just like her sister!

Catarina feels zero sympathy for Annie or Nicole. Most kids with unpredictable or absent parents come with bad habits. That's why orphans their age get tossed around from home to home. Nobody wants to put up with it! It's common knowledge that kids like Annie and Nicole, who have drug addicts as parents, mirror their actions. Just give it time.

People don't fully understand their situation. Since their arrival, the community expressed sympathy. "Poor girls" this and "poor girls" that! Catarina took it upon herself to invent stories about the girls. That way, she controlled the painting everyone saw. Instead of feeling sorry for *them*, Catarina's intent has always been to turn the remorse upon herself.

Thoughts, ideas, or any new way she can imagine reflecting the opposite of sweetness on the girls is her goal. The need to shame them, to tarnish their name, claws its way through Catarina's mind. *Just looking at their faces disgusts me!*

She grins at the priceless image of Annie's reaction to cat food. And then there are Catarina's brilliant performances when she would ask them nicely what they craved to eat. Most of the time, it was a cheeseburger.

But she never spent her hard-earned money on them. She bought the food per their request and indulged right in front of them, making both girls smell what they couldn't have. *As I always told them while enjoying my meal, they'll be able to buy as many cheeseburgers as they want the day they're out of my house. They should grovel for the food I offer them—ungrateful little parasites.*

Only a fool would believe Catarina could prefer another woman's children to her own. Women from the community like to say it all the time, "Oh, I would love them just like my own." But they wouldn't! That is an outright lie. A mother will always choose her biological child over any other.

Annie and Nicole may think Catarina is cold-hearted, but sometimes the truth is a harsh pill to swallow. She admits it's an ego boost to be noticed for looking after children who belong to no one. Constant public praise is a nice reward, especially when she announces their foster kid status to everyone around.

She loves the spotlight. When anything relates to Annie or Nicole, Catarina asks, "How can I make this about me?"

Nicole got to stay after Annie disappeared because Catarina has a kind heart. She told Santi Nicole could stay with them as long as they kept getting paychecks from the state. If she did not have a good heart, as everyone claims, she would have kicked Nicole to the curb along with Annie.

But Nicole had to pay her dues, too. She may be a teenager, but with Annie out of the way, Nicole needs to step up. Unfortunately, she isn't as talented as her big sister at evading detection. *I even had to work that cop over some with a little truth-stretching, so everything fell on Nicole. Now I've lost both their paychecks. Stupid girls. It's all Annie's fault.*

Catarina's seething thoughts of Annie turn to Gina, too. The girl always wants to defend that sorry waste of breath she considers her mother. Why doesn't she find her mom? Maybe they can be a big, happy family again. Maybe Annie will end up just like Gina—another junkie sporting a cardboard sign on some street corner.

Annie will never do better than being with Catarina. She bought them knock-off designer clothes and tried not to hit where bruises were visible—she knows how nosey people are. She always dressed them well, so nobody would judge her parenting.

A sinister grin separates Catarina's lips. *Usually, a solid flogging with a horsewhip while one of them took a shower gave me the satisfaction I needed. I kept them alive and taught them discipline so they wouldn't end up like their mother. How bad is that?*

Not having a job makes life at home boring, lonely, and sometimes too much for Catarina's mind to handle. Now that Nicole is gone, too, her idle hands and invasive thoughts need an outlet. She loses herself creating fake profiles, adding every person who knows Annie. She fabricates posts using curse words and works to portray the narrative of a rebellious, promiscuous, troubled teenage girl. No one will think Annie is so innocent now!

With Nicole in jail and Annie trying to navigate college, they might try running back to me for help. But I won't help either of them. No more! The way they came is the way they are going to leave! With nothing!!! If the paycheck isn't coming in for a lifetime, then it's easier to wash my hands clean from having them around me. Nobody likes junk. That's what these girls are to me—dirt beneath my shoe.

CHAPTER 22

Catarina's regret for taking in Annie and Nicole has become animosity and resentment. A whole lot of it, too. Annie's face repulses her. Nicole is merely tolerable and only because of the potential return of the income if she ever gets out of jail.

The attorney's office has been calling Catarina's phone all day. She doesn't have money to hire her own attorney, so she accepted her entitled free one. Hopefully, they will offer probation or something simple, like community service. She told them everything was Nicole's idea. Nicole called Catarina to pick her up from her friend Corine's house. She had no clue the girl had broken into any homes.

From the cop's reaction, she knew he believed the lies she fed him. The cops were asking if Nicole had mental issues and all sorts of questions. Catarina simply reiterated it was all Nicole's plan. There is no way Catarina will go to jail for this.

The detective, who was nothing like the first cop she spoke to, had it in for her. She still doesn't like his tone of voice or his threats of ten years behind federal prison bars. He claims evidence exists, threatening Catarina's downfall. His last warning haunts her even now.

"I'm going to take you down, Mrs. Coyazo, even if it is the last case I investigate before I retire. Mark my words, I will get to the bottom of this."

She reviews the entire conversation with the detective in her head. Catarina's mind is her usual dwelling place. But her imagined world is now becoming reality. The detective is pathetic if he thinks he has any evidence to arrest her. She watches enough documentaries to know they can only make an arrest if they have enough evidence. He has no proof. That's why he is threatening her into telling him the truth, but she's smart and has caught on to his little game. No, Catarina won't believe him for a second. Not a chance!

On her way to grab a value menu pizza, she rejects the detective's calls at least twice. She doesn't have time for him to figure her out, and she won't hand herself over, either. When she gets the chance, she will call him back. She pulls into the parking lot of the same plaza as the pizza joint. Shifting the gear into park, she walks into Lenny's Pawn Shop.

Catarina looks around the store, but nothing catches her eye today. She strolls up to the tall man standing behind the cash register. He seems young enough to think they are fake. *Yeah, I'm going to do it.*

Catarina walks back to her car to grab the earrings that once belonged to her best friend, Corine. The old woman must have thought Catarina would feel bad for her when she told her the news, but she just pretended to care and offered to give her a replacement pair of her own. Of course, that woman would wear nothing belonging to Catarina. She knew what she was doing.

The tall man behind the front counter glances up as she walks back inside. She makes eye contact and applies her best flirty tone. "You've got some good deals going on." She offers a quick wink. He is not the type of man she would ever pursue, but he is young enough to believe he can attract an older woman. Still, he ignores her comment.

She walks through one last aisle before sauntering up to the cash register. Catarina hands over the diamond earrings so the pawn shop employee can inspect them. The young man walks to the back area designated for employees only. He takes longer than five minutes back there, and her fingers fidget.

A small bell sits on the counter with a paper taped on it, asking patrons to ring the bell for service. She does just that, hoping someone comes out to help because that man probably took off with the earrings, for all she knows. Catarina rings the bell dramatically for the last time, and the same tall, young man returns to the front desk. She raises her right brow to show her angry impatience.

"I am sorry, ma'am, but I cannot give you the earrings back because..." Catarina interrupts the employee mid-sentence.

"You can't give them to me because of what?"

"Ma'am, like I was trying to say before you rudely interrupted, the police are on their way because the item you are attempting to pawn has been reported stolen."

"Oh, this is BS! Someone set me up!"

Catarina walks calmly out of Lenny's Pawn Shop, trying her best to avoid direct eye contact with their cameras. Who knows if they function, but she doesn't want to risk it. They can keep the earrings! The way she feels inside should ensure she never does that again. Her heart pounds out of her chest, and her hands won't stop shaking.

Catarina has trouble unlocking the car door. Did Annie and Nicole feel this way each time she sent them in to steal?

CHAPTER 23

S tern pounding accompanies a deep male voice shouting with authority at Catarina's front door.

"State Police, open up!"

The sound echoes through the quiet living room, and each strike on the door sounds with increased urgency. Her heart races as she senses the weight of the situation—it's not just one officer. Looking outside the living room blinds, it appears every officer on duty stands outside her door.

As Catarina peeps through the blinds, her gaze lands on a stern-looking woman in plain clothes, but she can see a badge gleaming from her waistband. Tension stretches across her face as she scans the front of their home with a vigilant gaze. The rich, authoritative voice calls out again with a greater sense of urgency.

"Ma'am, we know you're in there. We see you peeking through the blinds. You need to open up, or we will force entry. We have a warrant!"

Those words are frightening. She knows the severity of the situation now. They have it all twisted. If they think for a second that she's going to let this go without a fight, they're in for a rude awakening.

She turns around to find her daughter, Celi, in tears. Catarina's heart aches with longing to shield her from this. Nicole is in the county jail, and Annie is gone from the house, too. Even Santi is at away at work, leaving Celi as the only witness to her arrest. Knowing she sees is worse than impending imprisonment.

As Catarina wilts on the edge of this chaotic moment, her mind can't escape reality—this will affect Celi deeply. She wishes with all her heart she could shield her daughter from this pain. Maybe, just maybe, there's still a chance they'll believe the caring foster parent over the troubled foster kid. Catarina has often persuaded herself she's the better person. Surely they won't choose to believe the girl with no parents over someone who opened their home to two underprivileged kids.

But the truth is, Annie and Nicole were never naughty. She labeled them as such to evoke sympathy and convince others of the burden she carried. If she had spoken the truth—how they are well-behaved girls who help with chores, follow instructions, and don't talk back—people might view them as better than any of her own kids. No one can see Gina's daughters in a good light. Catarina must always be in control.

She rushes to the room to change her shirt. She'd rather they not arrest her in the one she wore to the pawnshop. A plain black t-shirt slips over her head as her arms push through untattered holes. She always knows how to find the nicest looking clothes. She tugs it down over her waistband and slowly unlocks the front door. Turning the doorknob, Catarina meets her dreaded fate.

"Catarina Linda Coyazo, you are being arrested on a felony charge for grand larceny, a felony for theft of property, and another felony charge of coercing a minor to commit a crime. You have the right to remain silent..."

Everything goes blank. Catarina extends her arms, feeling the yank from the female uniformed officer as she tightens the cold metal cuffs around her wrists. The icy steel pinches her skin, resignation falling over her features—no more fighting. A strange sense of vulnerability creeps in as the gravity of the situation pulls at Catarina's legs, making it difficult to stand. With each passing second, she prepares for the tidal wave of uncertainty roaring her way. *What did Nicole say for them to charge me with that last charge involving a minor? What does coercing a minor even mean? Did she say I...oh no! That girl is going to get it when I see her!*

From the back of the police car, Catarina sees Santi's work truck speeding up toward the front of the house. She knows him well enough to know he won't leave her after this. He is such a good man. Even if she is officially a felon after all this mess, and even if she has to spend a few days in jail, he is the type of man who stays, no matter what. *Shoot! He will go borrow the money to post my bond, so I won't even have to spend a single night in jail.* Three uniformed men keep him from approaching the vehicle where Catarina sits bound. One officer breaks away from the bunch and makes his way toward her.

"Alright, Mrs. Coyazo, we are ready to head out. Your husband has been notified of the situation." The officer with A. *Smith* engraved across a flashy badge uses a chill tone as he speaks to her through the grate separating them..

"Where are we going?" Tears linger on the rim of her lower lids.

"Downtown. We're booking you for the three felony charges."

The rest of the drive remains silent. She's learned firsthand what arrest entails. Handcuffs and a complimentary visit to the county jail, along with a criminal record. For a moment, the taste of karma moistens the inside of her mouth, a bitter reminder of the repercussions of her choices. At least revenge hits back ten times harder. It's Catarina's only satisfaction.

While sitting inside the county jail booking lobby, she realizes she is no better than any other person inside those cells. Everyone wears the same dull, orange-colored jumpsuit and endures their own struggles, bound by their shared humanity and the mistakes they've made. Catarina can see the stories etched in the surrounding faces, and it becomes clear they all deserve compassion and understanding, not judgment. The stark realization hits her. *Oh! Now I want grace. This is scary.*

Ironically, she lacks empathy and makes no genuine effort to care for others in most situations. She cares about herself and how she can be the victim in every scenario she finds herself. She also has a tendency to divulge every confidence and intimate detail ever shared with her—there are no secrets behind her lips other than her own. Emotions escalate from calm to explosive in seconds, shocking everyone around her. No one should share personal information with someone like Catarina. Once she senses the slightest hint of betrayal, disloyalty, or tension—game over.

Chapter 24

Catarina uses her one phone call to reach out to Santi. Knowing that hiring a private attorney is beyond her financial means, she accepts legal help from a public defender. After what feels like an eternity of ringing, the familiar click connects Catarina to her husband, who has generously paid to accept the call. She can almost picture him wincing at the thought of the phone charges, knowing the way her husband is with his money. The charge to speak to her injures his pockets.

He hates throwing away money. He never celebrates the Fourth of July holiday because he refuses to buy fireworks. Buying fireworks is equivalent to grabbing a crisp dollar bill and lighting it on fire. Each boom and sparkle, Santi insists, is just money going up in smoke, and he would rather save cash for something he deems worthwhile. The thought of wasting even a cent is enough to keep him grounded.

The thought of his frugal nature tugs at Catarina's heartstrings. His love for her drives him to accept this call despite the cost.

Santi promises to get her out of jail and confirms he has already posted the bond so they can release her.

"Where in the world did you get the money to post the bail so quickly?" Catarina only thought Santi's resourcefulness was without flaw.

"I leveraged the title of your car as collateral. The quick cash and loans establishment offers immediate cash for your vehicle's title. We have thirty days to repay the loan amount plus interest or they can repossess your car and keep it permanently."

She struggles to keep her emotions in check and not voice her frustration at his poor decision-making. Now, because of this reckless choice, they may have no other option but to turn to her sister or his family for help to cover the loan payment. Why couldn't he ask his rich sister for aid instead of taking the title to her car and pawning it? If they fail to repay his sister, she won't take the same measures as the loan company.

Catarina's credit is so bad, she couldn't finance a stick of gum, and it's irreparable at this point. At her age, she has no desire to improve the score, either. Renting suits her lifestyle just fine. Owning a house is just wishful thinking. Catarina's already screwed her credit before she met Santi. What he didn't know was *how* bad it was. She even resorted to using Santi's information to take out credit cards. When he found that out several months ago, he wasn't upset. He didn't even seem surprised about what she had done. He never acted like it bothered him.

Metallic clicks echo in the stark, sterile hallway as the guard turns his keys and opens the thick metal door with a creak. The corrections officer steps into view, intense authority oozing from the index finger he points down the hallway.

"Get up, Coyazo. You're up for questioning."

Catarina follows him to a room at the end of the dimly lit corridor.

It's difficult to walk when you're shackled from head to toe and on the heavier side of the scale. As they approach the interrogation room, an unfamiliar, heavy feeling settles in Catarina's stomach. The light flickers overhead, obscuring everything but a metal table in the center of the room where a detective sits across from an empty chair reserved for her. Doubts cloud her mind—there is no time to think of a way to escape this one.

Happy little Nicole, safely tucked away with the juveniles and probably enjoying a level of comfort I can only envy. Surely, her rights are more protected, given her age. Still, there is no sympathy in Catarina's heart for the girl. The world beyond these walls will be far more unforgiving. If Nicole thinks for a second this is tough, she can't imagine what is coming next for her.

Life has a silly way of teaching us hard lessons, and Catarina has no intention of sugarcoating it for her. The girl will never see it coming!

CHAPTER 25

When Catarina first took us in, she let me join the cheerleading squad, allowed Nicole to play basketball like she always wanted to, and even gifted me a phone. I thought I had the most extraordinary life during the first few months with the Coyazos. I wasn't even ten years old, and I had my own cell phone! A knock-off designer purse made others think I was living my best life.

All along, I used materialistic items to mask the pain, manipulation, and deceit happening behind closed doors. Perhaps the church believed her web of lies. Maybe even the community believed her false narrative. But I knew the truth about her.

She was manipulative. That first year and every year after, she took our Christmas gifts from the annual Angel Tree ministry. This is a program specifically designed for foster children, and it offers the community a chance to fulfill desired Christmas wishes for a child they select from the tree. Her voice grates in my inner ear even now.

"I put a Versace perfume on the list, so if anyone gets it for you, it's mine."

When I opened my mouth to protest the unfairness, she made it clear with a light threat, insisting she would take away my phone and pawn it to buy the perfume. She claimed I wanted to give her attitude. I wasn't doing that, though. It just seemed unjust.

Her love, her time, even the food in our mouths came at a price. Catarina was meticulous about her strategy and plan. If I wanted to go out to eat with them, I had to fork over my portion of the cash to cover half of the entire family's meal.

This didn't happen in the beginning. At first, everything was great. It almost felt too good to be living. From a local store's changing room to an actual bed, it feels fraudulent when you're used to nothing.

But living with a narcissistic foster mother felt like a daily mental battlefield—always in fight-or-flight mode. No child should go through that. I was already in a state of survival when she brought us into her home. Developing the essential skills of outsmarting my abuser became an unwelcome challenge. When I noticed she found pleasure in hitting me and watching me cry, I stopped crying.

Even though I continued to forgive her questionable behavior, I hoped she would change. The day I no longer craved her affection or approval, the intense longing for love faded like a distant memory. I endured enough pain to detangle myself from the habit of needing motherly advice. I accepted Catarina's love came with conditions. Everything she felt came at a price. Her advice, tainted with condescension, wasn't even genuine.

With time and a lot of therapy, I unfurled my attachments to her daughters. Their mother's web of lies entangled them, too, despite their apparent innocence. I didn't wish her harm. All I ever hoped for Catarina Coyazo was a discovery of her true self reflected in an encounter with someone else. That doesn't seem too harsh, simply hoping for the day she meets herself in another.

I cannot escape the haunted moments as a child yearning for a parent's love, affection, and unwavering support. Instead, I received only distance. The Coyazos taking Nicole and me in meant they would love us like their own, or at least help mend the shattered pieces of our hearts. How wrong I was. Both about them and the vision constructed in my mind.

I know it seems trivial, but there were times Catarina would take a weekend trip to the small Mexican town just beyond the border, spending nearly a hundred dollars to get us clothes and some knock-off purses. In contrast, her children enjoyed the luxury of shopping at the local malls.

Everyone returned to school from summer vacation in August. Catarina and Santiago would take the time to get their daughter, Celi's, school supplies and clothes months in advance, but they left Nicole and me scrambling a week before classes began. Celi had options with her school supplies, but few choices remain when you're getting everything at the last minute and the shelves are half empty.

My foster mother did not allow me to take a backpack to school. Catarina insisted I carry my textbooks in the knock-off designer purse she found in Mexico. Carrying all those heavy books in a shoulder bag left residual weight on my shoulders–a lingering reminder of the mental anguish and emotional toll of unfulfilled expectations.

The narrative was merely a façade that Catarina meticulously crafted for the world to see. No one acknowledged my truth. Not even the case worker when I confided in her about Catarina's betrayal—how she misappropriated the clothing vouchers intended for my sister and me. Instead of using those vouchers to provide us with clothes, Catarina claimed them for her other children, whose wardrobes were already overflowing. They wore nice new shoes each school year, leaving Nicole and me with scraps.

It's not that I'm ungrateful. It's simply my time to share my side without catering to anyone else's expectations. The Coyazos believed covering us with knock-off designer clothing would hide the scars or somehow convince others we were well-cared for.

At least now, I understand designer labels, even the fake version, do not imply love from the provider of such luxuries. Uttering the words I *love you* is simple, but actions of care and commitment reflect true love. I don't doubt the Coyazos love their daughters. However, they never extended the same unconditional love to Nicole or me. Instead, Catarina seized an opportunity, exploited it, and washed her hands.

To genuinely love a child is to nurture and protect them. Period.

Chapter 26

The first time Santiago shared his wife's inefficiency with meeting his needs, I was too young and naïve to comprehend his meaning. I walked into their room to turn in my unlocked phone—a nightly obligation regardless of whether it was a weekend or school night. Out of the corner of my eye, confusing images splayed across the screen. There was far too little clothing, and somehow, I knew it felt wrong. He quickly mashed the power button, simultaneously dropping a towel in his lap. That was odd.

I tried to avoid eye contact when I placed my device on their nightstand, as if handing over a prized possession. It had to be in its place by the designated time—no exceptions. Catarina would knock me into next week if I kept it a second too long, even if she wasn't home to witness my delayed obedience.

Santiago cleared his throat and called me to his side.

"Do you want a little extra phone privilege this weekend?"

I didn't really know how to answer. Obviously, I coveted phone time so I could talk with Chasity—to have some sense of normalcy in my life. But things like that always had a price. I'd already given so many disgusting foot massages and hairy back rubs to last a lifetime. I did it so Nicole didn't have to, but tonight, I really didn't want to again.

The stifling air in the room couldn't mask the awkwardness growing between us.

"Catarina is a busy woman, you know. She doesn't always have time to fulfill all her wifely responsibilities." His eyes shifted to the now darkened computer screen before turning back to meet mine with a new hunger in them I couldn't fully describe.

I felt an overwhelming need to escape, but Catarina wasn't home, so I couldn't even feign excuses of her ordering me to clean. He said he felt bad about it, but he couldn't help it. His wife wasn't getting the job done.

I dared not move, as his whisper violated my ear and his meaty hand reached for my thigh.

"Don't worry. Catarina knows all about this. That's why she left us alone."

Tears streamed unbidden down my face as six-year-old me heard my uncle's compliments in the deep recesses of my mind. "So *young. Oh so beautiful,*

Sweetie." The memory assaulted me as deeply as Santiago did in that moment.

Pain isn't always a physical beating. Sometimes, it's a man gutting a little girl's innocence—leaving wounds never to be seen but forever felt.

My childhood bed was never a safe place to sleep. My uncle would go to great lengths to get me alone. He called it my "cookie" like it was some innocent nickname—our twisted, secret code. But when I screamed at everyone, the only way I knew how, "HE TOUCHED MY COOKIE!" nobody listened. They didn't understand.

Disguising evil as a word sweet enough to silence suspicion—he would do anything to keep his secret safe. If I ever have a little girl, I promise to teach her the appropriate terms for every body part. I will never ignore a child's silent cry for help.

Receiving a compliment from a guy meant he desired me. I know where this distorted belief originated. Being complimented as a little girl while unspeakable atrocities took place under the covers definitely made me question my self-worth, and it was all somehow tied to the attention of others. No child should blame themselves for the actions of their abuser!

Yet Catarina's words invade my mind like a searing reminder of the pain inside me. My understanding of affection's connection to being wanted is troubling. Even after all these years, I still grapple with the horrible memory of her disgusting notion. "A *man only goes as far as a woman lets him.*"

That concept is utterly inaccurate, especially with children. They lack the emotional tools needed to navigate such a complicated dynamic. So, yes, my heart continues to ache for the little girl I was—trapped in a maze of adult concepts that should never have applied.

Santiago Coyazo. Everyone sees a perfect father and husband, but I know the truth. He is no better than my uncle. He is a straight-up pig. I would voluntarily submit to a lie-detector test on national television any day and answer ONE question to reveal the intentions of the monster who carries that name.

"Did Santiago Coyazo ever rape you?"

Yes. Yes, he did.

Chapter 27

Nicholas A. Ferroni once said, *"Students who are loved at home, come to school to learn, and students who aren't, come to school to be loved."*

The trouble at home, living with Catarina, was why school was my favorite place to be. I cherish the transformative essence of education, recognizing it as the key to unlocking new opportunities and reshaping our futures. Where I come from, people like me don't make it to college. Most are proud to receive their high school diploma. It satisfies their hunger for success.

For others, going to college is never an option. Receiving a college education is a privilege for the wealthy, but for people who come from broken homes, it's a luxury. Born into a family that fails to appreciate my presence and overlooks my value, growing up with abusive foster parents, dealing with physical and psychological trauma after trauma all taught me those pieces of pain are forever part of me. Many may be terrifying shards, but they are mine, and I refuse to take them for granted.

It's just past midnight, when a dense fog of writer's block settles over me. My cluttered desk, where stacks of textbooks and crumpled notes stifle my creativity, distracts me from diving into a research paper for my science class. The motivation to begin is nowhere to be found, just like my parents. Just kidding!

This assignment feels like a chore, struggling against the current of my thoughts. The word hate feels too intense, particularly in a world already burdened with enough negativity. Perhaps I should say I intensely dislike writing. Initially, I envisioned starting the paper with a whimsical *once upon a time*, but it seems the rules prohibit such an opening in bold, capitalized letters. Why must college be so difficult?

The research paper involves detailing my family tree, but the mere thought of tracing my ancestry is laughable. I can only outline my estranged mother and father and maybe her mother, but I know absolutely nothing about where I come from—so humiliating! I don't have many gaps to fill where the connections should be because it's Nicole and me. That's it. That's how it's always been. And right now, even that feels frail.

I considered adopting a dog from the local shelter several times, but I can't afford another mouth to feed. Also, I don't want a dog simply because the furry companion will ease my loneliness. That would be equivalent to people who have kids to fix their troubled marriage or because they think a tiny human will fill the emptiness inside of them. Don't they know you can't pour from an empty cup?

An eternity passes while I stare at the screen, displaying nothing but my name, the date, my professor's name, and the title of my paper. This is all so isolating! The blank page reflects my own doubts and insecurities, an internal yearning to express something meaningful, yet an invisible barrier blocks me.

I'm not a writer. I can't just create stories in my head and type them onto a computer screen. My brain doesn't function that way. I'm remarkable at mathematics. I have always enjoyed it, even as an underclassman taking a calculus class among the juniors and seniors in high school.

I must get through college because I owe it to her—the girl with no family.

It's probably not healthy to reflect on so many of the traumatizing parts of my life. Mental instability would take over without the ability to confide in Mitsy about Catarina or without Chasity's genuine support. Girls my age are unkind. Still, hearing genuine compliments from other women feels validating and authentic.

Anytime a guy compliments me, I can't help but think he has ulterior motives. No one knows those thoughts exist. I've kept them locked away, never articulated my entire life. However, I have a creeping suspicion Chasity pieced it together years ago. She has always been curious about the unusual and unsettling rules surrounding my interactions with Santiago Coyazo.

In this tangled web of secrecy, Chasity was my sole confidant. She never ridiculed me or judged my weird, toxic situation. Chasity's genuine friendship embraced me with understanding, never once humiliating me about what I endured. That is why we have remained friends all this time. Chasity is the companion God knew my heart needed in my most desperate moments.

When the Coyazos periodically kicked me out, I wandered the sidewalk, lost, with no place to go. Chasity never pried or bombarded me with questions. Instead, she offered her family home and reassured me all would be okay. I miss those moments under the comforting umbrella of her family.

I pick up my phone and text her the words coming straight from my heart: *I love you. Miss you bunches!* XOXO. Before I hit send, the message feels incomplete without an emoji to capture the emotion I hope to convey. I scroll through the options and choose the yellow heart, a piece of my affection. Our friendship is a tribute to our high school memories and the color of sunshine suits it well.

I am fully aware of the few loose screws upstairs, but I question whether my sanity would hold without these girls as my outlet. As another escape for my mental health, I started going on walks around a neighborhood near campus.

At first, I thought this quiet, quaint residential area was an elderly living facility because the well-built houses are in a gated community. They prompt my curiosity regarding their inhabitants' professions. On my walks, I play a guessing game to imagine what the person in each home does for a living. Most of my answers steer toward a doctor, a lawyer, maybe a plastic surgeon in between, or some luxury real estate agent.

An incoming call from Mitsy disrupts my internal game. Before I can even say hello, her rapid-fire question launches through the earpiece.

"Hey, I'm gonna grab food. Want anything?"

"I appreciate you thinking of me, but I've gotta get a lot done before I can head back to our room."

"Well, okay then. Enjoy your walk around the rich people's neighborhood." How does her voice chirp like that? "Oh! Before I hang up, which one are you exploring today?"

I stop to gulp ice-cold water while we chat and tell her all about this fancy little community. Mitsy's giddiness matches mine, and I embrace the support of another loyal friend and the best roommate, too!

Recently, Mitsy has been the only person there for me, so meeting a stranger during my walk this afternoon is a welcome blessing. I find a dog, and I want to keep him. HE IS SO CUTE. His name is Petey, according to the engraved tag hanging from a blue collar around his tiny neck. He is a cute dog with a cute name. I march toward the address on his collar, contemplating pets in general. I have never owned one.

Catarina always considered dogs dirty and stinky, even though she kept a big dog outside. It lived there in the scorching heat and the blistering cold. The poor dog ended up losing its life to some illness, never confirmed. Santiago and Catarina said it was parvo. I lean toward negligence.

The numbers on the next house shake me from my thoughts. This is it. Walking up to the decorated porch, I admire the decor surrounding the home. It's perfect.

Also, I was way off on my guess of how the owners of this home look. The enormous ebony door opens to a brunette talking a hundred miles per second on the phone. The beautiful woman does not seem shocked that a total stranger is handing over her lost dog. She shows off her perfect teeth—a purchased smile. The woman is striking. I don't wait long as she quickly ends her phone call.

"Oh, thank you! My little Petey is quite the rascal!"

She smiles again while reaching out to grab the tiniest, most adorable little dog I've ever held. I attempt subtlety as I crane my neck to peer inside this woman's home. Her exterior decorating screams interior design expertise, and I wonder what artistry lies behind her open door.

A path of solar lights lines her sidewalk. The porch decor is the kind you screenshot online to use as an inspirational picture. The outside of her house alerts any guest that spring is near. Colorful tulips surround the front lawn filled with random bunnies, eggs, and Easter reminders.

The fragrance escaping her home smells like a hug. I don't even know how to describe it. It's clean, but also something bakes in the oven, and out of my peripheral vision, I see bright yellow lemonade in a glass pitcher on the kitchen island.

"Would you like to come in? Maybe have some freshly squeezed lemonade or a cup of organic iced tea?"

I'm not sure what organic iced tea tastes like, but the fact that it's iced is enough for me to accept this stranger's generous offer with gladness. Stepping across her threshold, I realize it doesn't feel like a house. The ambiance, warmth, and tranquility make this place different. It feels like a home.

Before I know it, I'm two hours deep into a trauma dump with a total stranger while drinking the best iced tea.

CHAPTER 28

I 've lost track of time. I honestly don't know what hour it is. The thought of walking over a mile back to the campus dorms in the dark isn't comforting. While the remarkable woman I spent the afternoon with is incredibly kind, she has a bit of a bossy streak.

In just a few hours, I've discovered two things about her. She has extensive knowledge of many things and rarely sugarcoats her thoughts. Her name, Sylvia Gilly, has a lovely ring to it, and I wonder whether Gilly is her maiden name or her husband's.

I dream of changing mine someday when I finally learn how to navigate the process legally. I hate sharing the last name of a man I have never met.

The jingling keys take me straight back to Catarina's chilling voice, hollering through the house. "*Let's go!*" After which, she forced Nicole and me to break into houses to steal for her or lift random items from the department store so she could sell them.

Sylvia's authoritative voice, laced with a touch of sass, drags me from my momentary nightmare.

"If you thought for a second that I was going to let you walk back by yourself in the dark, you have lost your God-given mind."

We walk out the front door into brilliant moonlight. I hop right into Mrs. Gilly's enormous vehicle. For a woman as petite and elegantly composed as Sylvia, I instinctively placed her in a luxury vehicle, perhaps a sleek BMW that embodies her sense of style. Instead, I launch myself into a towering 4x4 truck, reaching for the sturdy grab bar to help me into the passenger seat.

Mrs. Gilly turns into the campus parking lot and hands me her phone number, neatly written on a flowered napkin. I cradle the paper in my palm, the significance of her gesture surprising me. She has been kind to me, and I acknowledge the flutter of appreciation swelling within. In mere hours, this woman wove a tapestry of warmth around me, enveloping me in a love I have never experienced before.

We exchange goodbyes, and I close the door to Mrs. Gilly's vehicle.

Walking toward my dorm room, I look for the moon in the inky sky. The city is unusually dark tonight. Clouds obscure the stars but do not dull the shine reflecting from the full moon. My favorite scent creates a fragrance that awakens my senses. The smell of rain invigorates me with peace I can't explain.

I've heard whispers that Seattle has a high depression rate, linked to the city's infamous gray skies. But it baffles me how rain—something so soothing to me—brings overwhelming sadness for others. For me, rain is a gentle healer. It eases the unspoken burdens weighing heavily on me.

I slowly unlock the door to my dorm, and a wave of guilt washes over me, puncturing the calm façade I tried to maintain throughout the years. It settles deep in my gut as I envision Nicole's life interrupted far too soon. She wasn't even able to attend high school, to receive a diploma, and now she faces the grim reality of spending the next decade in a cold, unforgiving cell.

I am confident nobody leaves this world without someone balancing the scales of justice, even if it takes time. Revenge is a dangerous path, and though anger simmers just beneath the surface, I know better than to let negative feelings consume me. Taking matters into my own hands would only lead to more chaos and pain. Sometimes, the most powerful action is inaction. As infuriating as it may be, the best response is often stepping back and allowing life to unfold as it will.

I open my phone camera while lying in bed. I never take a soft place to rest for granted, ever. Even reclining here now feels fraudulent and wrong. I feel guilty because only God knows if Nicole has a clean bed to sleep in tonight. Uncontrollable tears give way to dramatic sobbing as I stare at the photo of my sister and me.

"Annie, are you okay? What's wrong?"

Mitsy's soft voice conveys genuine sadness as she jumps out of her bed, tosses the pillows aside, and rushes into the bathroom. Mitsy returns with a handful of tissues and leans in to comfort me with a hug.

I show her the video saved on my phone of Catarina unknowingly admitting to what she was planning on telling the cops. *"You know, Nicole is a minor. They will remove the charges by the time she is an adult. It will be off her record. But me? If I get caught and tell the truth that it was me, they will put me in jail for a long time. So, Nicole is just gonna have to eat this charge without choking."* Catarina is a cold-blooded psychopath.

"Wait, wait, go back and replay that part. What in the world did she just say?"

Mitsy wavers between shock, confusion, and even a hint of disgust in her voice. As we replay the video for the fourth time, nausea once again crashes over me.

Each replay of the video amplifies the familiar, unsettling feeling that occurs when dealing with someone who lashes out in anger, expecting everything to revert to normal, like their hurtful words never left their lips. Countless times I took her backhanded comments, physical lashings, and an endless amount of emotional blows, all because of that woman's deep-rooted insecurities which fed my own.

The extreme mental push and pull, the constant highs and lows of her emotional roller coaster, left me reeling. I constantly walked on eggshells, perpetually bracing for the next emotional blow. Each toxic explosion chipped away at my sense of self, and to this day, it's exhausting to think about the effects of navigating life with a narcissist.

CHAPTER 29

T o my biological parents, wherever you are, if you ever read this, I don't hate you. I just hate the pain I had to go through because of you.

As I navigate young adulthood, the complexity of relationships reiterates the importance of creating boundaries. Ms. Gigi, as she prefers to be called, has profoundly influenced my understanding of mental health. She is not your average therapist. Her genuine compassion, insight, and unwavering support have transformed my past perspective into healing.

There are countless moments when I seek Ms. Gigi's companionship rather than formal therapy. I don't always need to share my feelings with a therapist in a clinical setting or a family member whose advice often comes with a bias. Our relationship is a comforting friendship. Ms. Gigi has the gift of listening to others with an open heart.

Do you know how rare that is nowadays? She has an extraordinary ability to listen to me on a deeper level and always makes me feel heard and understood.

I don't need to be strong in her office. I can just be me. Her understanding, mental health support, and genuine care for her patients is on a level that surpasses any typical client-therapist relationship.

Ms. Gigi's advice this time is to go "no contact" for thirty days with my abuser. Our therapy sessions have taught me the effects of abuse don't always show off in a physical form. Sometimes, abuse is a mental anguish you can't escape. A torment of constant reminders. *You are nobody. You're never going to be anybody.*

Well, look at me now—living and thriving without anyone's suffocation.

Deep-seated anger toward Catarina is inevitable. In fact, anger is an understatement. I feel full-blown animosity. Catarina placed my baby sister in an appalling predicament. In turn, I've hit rock bottom, trapped in a cycle of despair and helplessness.

My only solace comes from the prospect of visiting Nicole across a cafeteria table with guards and cameras scrutinizing every action and word we share, where she faces the grim realities of life as a habitual offender.

Nicole, a girl who has never even taken an extra piece of candy for herself and has always been the epitome of innocence, is now labeled a habitual offender—an individual arrested several times for crimes like robbery and burglary. Of course, anyone who commits a crime should face the consequences, but what happens when those criminal actions, especially as a child, arise solely from the coercion and manipulative instruction of the person who is supposed to be your parent?

You may think, "Why didn't you just say no?" But we couldn't. You can't understand unless you have lived with someone like Catarina.

Under her roof, I witnessed firsthand the severe repercussions for anything she deems disobedience. Being anywhere near that woman is stifling. Her actions trapped my sister in a situation that seems almost impossible to escape. I have been there before.

I can't even take a shower anymore without the fear of someone walking in and whipping me—her way of making sure we couldn't get away from her sadistic punishment. She kept us psychologically caged. If Nicole and I refused her commands, the coming pain better not surprise us.

It's my fault Nicole and I faced discipline in the shower. I tried to outsmart Catarina when I knew a potential beating was coming. How silly of me to even think that! She was bigger and smarter than me.

When she warned me she would have a field day teaching me respect, I panicked. I grabbed a handful of her maxi pads and lined my underwear. Surely it would work to provide a little cushion so it wouldn't hurt as badly, but it didn't—not at all.

When Catarina realized I didn't react when she whipped my rear end but jumped in agonizing pain when the thick leather belt hit the side of my thigh, she had me strip down. That's when she discovered the pads. Catarina forced me to remove every piece of garment from my body and threw me outside. That night, I learned never to think I could outsmart a narcissist, never to take a bed for granted, and never to go against Catarina's orders.

Few people knew the extent of our abuse. The Coyazos' older daughter, Jen, was nice when we first moved in. She lived somewhere else and visited at will. I'm sure she had her own reasons for staying away, but she came around to give her baby a relationship with her grandmother.

Jen was always kind, but I don't think she knows the gifts her daughter got from her mother were almost all stolen. When months passed without a visit, or Catarina sensed a strain on their relationship, she would call her daughter to tell her she had some things for the baby.

I doubt Jen even knew that version of her mother, but I sure did. I even knew Catarina fled from a small town several years ago because she would write checks to people, knowing there was no money in the account. The local seller would later discover her theft after the check bounced. Social media was not popular back then, or else multiple people would have plastered her face throughout all the local buy-and-sell pages.

Catarina's true nature, the one Jen was clueless of, unfolded spectacularly when I was about twelve years old. She confidently instructed me to accompany her to a local children's clothing store, since she expected Jen to visit soon. She grabbed a hand-held basket, quickly filling it with her chosen items, including several pairs of pajamas, some shoes, a few t-shirts, and various accessories.

Once the stuff in the basket satisfied her, she gave me explicit orders. "Walk out of the store with the entire basket, and everything I put in better be in there! Not a single thing better fall out! I'll know alright." Her emphasis on "I'll know" left no room for doubt.

I understood she expected me to follow her instructions without questioning. However, Catarina didn't provide any guidance on what to do if a worker stopped me. Had she done so, I would have been prepared for what happened next.

Just as I was making my way to the exit, a man in plain, casual clothes intercepted me. Unknown to me, the store's security guard was monitoring the in-store cameras from the back room, ready to intervene.

The security guard's pupils were dark as his raised brow left no empathy for the mess unfolding before him. He eyed me with cold suspicion, convinced I was colluding with Catarina. I could see the news byline. *In a carefully orchestrated shoplifting scheme, a scholar teenager, who has never even thought about breaking the law, is somehow in on the plot.* Talk about irony!

Yes, it might have seemed like a well-thought-out plan, but the truth was far different. I was just a kid swept up in something much more significant than me.

Catarina, the adult who led me into this predicament, had manipulated me into her ruse. Her carefully designed scheme was unsuccessful. Her plan involved the theft of hundreds of dollars of children's items. Even though she was the one putting the items into the basket, I was the one who got arrested. Because Catarina did not leave the store with the stolen items, they didn't charge her. I was the thief.

I felt a deep sense of injustice as they handcuffed and placed me in the cold backseat of a police car. Frigid metal pressed against my wrists as the reality of my situation sank in. The security guard had a duty to protect the store from criminal activity, theft included. He had no choice but to contact the authorities to report the crime.

I was unaware the security guard would be the one to make sure they didn't book me for the crime. As I sat across from the detective that day, I unburdened myself. I laid out every detail, recounting the events leading up to the theft, and I insisted if he just took a moment to look at my phone, he would find a trove of evidence—text messages, photos, and plans—that exposed Catarina's twisted schemes. She'd manipulated me, playing on my naivete, while I had no idea I was being drawn into a crime that would leave me trapped in a web of consequences far beyond my control.

The detective believed me. Released without further questioning was grand news, but I was in for a rude awakening the moment I stepped foot into Catarina's home.

Chapter 30

For over six long months during my senior year of high school, I found myself in a digital desert, completely cut off from any access to my phone. Catarina, my strict guardian, confiscated it and imposed such a prolonged restriction it became a frequent topic of gossip among my classmates. Their sarcastic smirks and questions triggered embarrassment.

"Why such a long phone punishment?"

"Wow! What did you do to lose your phone for *such* a long time?"

"Did you see that post about...oh yeah, you don't have a phone!"

Phones are an essential tool, but they held more of an attraction back when smartphones were just entering mainstream culture. The thrill of ownership my friends first had when they showed off their new devices made my situation even more challenging.

To make matters even worse, Catarina resorted to unplugging the Wi-Fi, effectively locking me out of the vast online resources I relied on for school. Any work had to be done within school hours, where they limited access to shared computers and the occasional library visit.

Lunch was the only time I could access the internet for assignments. I always appreciated homework on paper. If it had to be done online, I had to grab a free lunch tray and then squeeze in all of my homework while eating. The library prohibited food and drinks, but the school librarian must have made an exception because she never asked me to leave.

Even activities that should have been simple pleasures, like attending school functions, were subject to Catarina's stringent conditions. I knew I would have to prove myself worthy of each event, whether that meant completing extra chores, rubbing Santiago's feet for an additional hour, or making Catarina happy with suggesting a trip to the "store" since I knew it was her favorite activity. I earned every privilege she gave me.

Most of the time, I forfeited events rather than face the burden of working for them, making a conscious decision to uphold my integrity. As a result, I skipped out on all the major celebrations—prom, homecoming, and the myriad of other senior activities. The only exception was the senior sunset, a cherished event I attended with my best friend, Chasity.

However, that unforgettable evening soured faster than milk left in a car under the scorching desert sun. Upon returning home, Catarina punished me harshly for being late—two minutes, to be precise. You might think any child arriving even a minute past curfew deserves a reprimand for causing worry. I understand that viewpoint. However, this situation was different. She punished me not for any reckless behavior, but for making her wait.

Those two insignificant minutes resulted in a uniquely severe penalty, forever etched in my memory.

"Since you think you know it all, just watch and see what happens."

Her words burned with a stinging memory of the life I lived for most of my childhood. I won't go into the gruesome details, but suffice it to say there was cat food involved, and Catarina didn't own a cat.

There were times Catarina seemed to try. She fed Nicole and me, provided us both with a roof over our heads, clothed us, and took us to doctors' appointments if we needed medical attention.

Of course, there was also the time the doctor visit ended at a mental institution where she claimed I was hearing and seeing things and shooting up illicit substances. She listed a plethora of mental issues, too. A few days of overnight observation and a negative drug test authorized my release back to Catarina. She insisted I tell them I was still hearing things in hopes they would keep me longer, but they prescribed me an anti-psychotic medication and sent me on my way.

Eventually, I started believing the lies the narcissist fed me. I followed her lead. Whatever Catarina wanted done, I did. As time passed, I increasingly yielded to her directives, surrendering my sense of reality to align with Catarina's perspective. It's remarkable how, in such scenarios, one can internalize the falsehoods propagated by someone else.

Catarina often portrayed herself as good-hearted, emphasizing her desire to help others and claiming to have the best intentions toward *all* her kids. However, I firmly believe genuine kindness and compassion cannot coexist with manipulative schemes that exploit and distort the truth. You're either a good person or you're not.

Catarina's indecent behavior included making me a scapegoat for her crimes. With me gone, Nicole has become her next victim. She was supposed to keep us away from pain, not put us in harm's way. I still feel the impact of every traumatic moment—the unimaginable consequences of rejecting her demented requests.

If only I had someone to shield me from this pain.

But when I ran away the last time, when I moved on with my life, I thought about myself. I didn't think about Nicole. The moment I found a way to shield my vulnerable self from an inevitable felony charge, I unwittingly put Nicole in harm's way. She is the one who ultimately took the brunt of the Coyazo's abuse.

Catarina forever altered her life while I'm left grappling with the guilt of my choice. I knew the consequences if I took the heat for our foster mother, but I don't know why I didn't think to just stay back with Nicole. I guess, deep down, I didn't expect Catarina to make such a young girl take the fall for everything.

I will strive so hard to transform myself into someone of value, someone capable of aiding others in situations like hers. That may be a daunting task to some, but it's something I embrace wholeheartedly. I love helping others who need a hand, even those who are undeserving. That's when grace kicks in.

I don't aspire to be wealthy. The allure of material possessions holds little to no interest for me. My genuine desire is to provide support and guidance for people who find themselves without a safety net. I've heard people say that it takes a village, but what do you do when you have none?

An epiphany sparks in my mind—maybe I'll create my own!

CHAPTER 31

M rs. Gilly invited me for coffee this morning. The problem—I strongly dislike coffee. The taste is unappealing, the rancid smell is revolting, and the dark brown color of the drink is not appetizing at all, regardless of how it's prepared. I also have a genuine concern about stained teeth, which is why I avoid sodas, dark-colored beverages, and smoking.

The smell of cigarettes is worse than coffee, and don't get me started on the air pollution from burning tobacco. I abhor cigarettes. I don't like to use the word hate, but I know why I despise them so much. Catarina smoked nearly two packs a day.

Glancing out the window, I notice storm clouds forming in the distance. My mind drifts to a different type of turbulence—a storm I wish I could forget.

Clouds hung heavy in the sunlit sky, a gentle breeze entered through cracks in the windows, and rain fell throughout the day. Catarina felt defeated as the weather prevented her trip to the corner store for cigarettes. I am almost certain if kids could purchase tobacco, she would have forced one of us to get them for her. Even in the pouring precipitation!

Catarina was off her rocker. I had never seen a person act like that. She was throwing things across the house, slamming cabinets, screaming as loud as possible. Any violence, you name it, and she was doing it. She became completely unhinged—so badly she yanked out her own hair like her thoughts were too loud to bear!

I made the mistake of asking if I should clean up the mess. Why didn't I know better? Maybe I was just a naïve teenager, still believing kindness could calm her storm. But Catarina didn't care about my age—or my heart. Eyes wild, she turned and smacked me across the cheek. Once. Twice. Again. Until my ears rang and I stopped counting.

"If you already know what you gotta do, don't you ever ask again if it's gotta get done!"

Then came the grab. She seized Nicole and me by the ears like we were nothing more than mutts, and dragged us into her room.

That's when I heard it.

The clink of metal chains.

Not ropes or belts. Chains. Heavy, frigid, real. I didn't know whether to cry or throw up. My heart plunged into my stomach. I glanced at Nicole. Her eyes, brimming with terror, bounced between the door and me. I offered a small nod, trying to reassure her it would be okay. But even as I did, I knew I was lying.

Catarina removed the lid from a permanent marker and the pungent chemical odor invaded my nostrils. An X for each time I neglected her command to "bark" wet my forehead. Each mark equaled impending punishment. She was far from finished.

My arms buckled under the weight of my body as my chin struck the floor. I swallowed the metallic taste of blood, wiping it from my split chin. Her silence was eerie. Normally, Catarina would be screaming, her angry spittle flying from her reddened face. But this time, her darkened eyes spoke volumes.

My body begged me to cower, but I knew Nicole was still in the room, and so I endured whatever came. My frame was not as frail as hers. It could withstand the force of Catarina's brutal kicks.

A presence brushed against me like the breeze outside the closed windows. It wrapped around my body as I instinctively curled into the fetal position. Despite the pounding in my head and aching around my ribs, I felt a soothing warmth as I disconnected from what was happening to me.

My mind failed to understand what my body felt when it connected with the wall on the other side of the room. Every breath brought excruciating pain.

The fire radiating from my bruised side was a stark contrast to the invisible gust of wind that brushed across my face, drying my tears.

My foster mother smoked three cigarettes as she repeatedly launched her foot directly into my tailbone. How do I know the exact number? Because Catarina Coyazo used my knees to extinguish every single one!!!

Thunder crashes with a flash of lightning, bringing me back to the present as a solitary tear escapes down my cheek. The same presence envelops me now, and I realize that even in the darkest of storms, I was never alone.

The rumbling of my stomach reminds me I have yet to eat—or text Mrs. Gilly back. Maybe I'll try something new this morning. I want to go over to Mrs. Gilly's and attempt to enjoy a cup of coffee with her. She could make a lovely addition to my village.

My last visit with her was some time ago when she gave me a ride back to the dorms so I wouldn't walk alone in the dark. She texts me to check in on me, and I like it when she reaches out. Those thoughtful gestures make my day so much brighter! She even gave me a spare key a few weeks ago so I could keep an eye on her plants while she was away on vacation.

Following instructions when tending her plants prevents upsetting her. Silvia Gilly loves her plants. In any way the plant may come, she adores them! I don't care for plants or flowers much, but for Mrs. Gilly, I have learned to tend to them like newborn babies.

While watering the outdoor plants, I got to admire the beauty found in the colors within the boundaries of her backyard. Apart from being spacious, it looks like it belongs in the pages of an interior design magazine. The colors of each flower belong in the place where they grow. She planted the lemon trees strategically for optimal sunshine, and the blossoming tulips complement every corner of her backyard. It will be nice to see those blooms today.

I wipe my face with a makeup remover towel and apply dark brown mascara to my eyelashes. The rich, earthy hue makes my ocean-blue eyes sparkle differently. Because my skin is porcelain, black mascara makes me look more gothic, and I prefer a softer look.

I don't much care to look at the girl in the mirror right now, so after quickly smearing gloss across my thin lips, I close my compact mirror and shove it right back into my cheetah print makeup bag. Zipping up the cheaply made bag, I toss it onto the bed I always make before starting my day.

The chore is as second-nature as if a drill sergeant hammered it into me. I don't do it because anyone forced me to growing up. Every morning, I make my bed because of this video I watched online where a man discussed the importance of making your bed and its impact on success. I appreciate it most when my days are crumbling apart or I have worked on my feet for over eight exhausting hours. To come home to a neatly made bed is such a blessing.

I appreciate my twin-sized bunk bed more than a newly purchased pair of shoes, an expensive designer purse, or whatever college kids are into nowadays. No one in my small group of friends appreciates their bed. I have heard nothing more than complaints—beginning with its size. Most kids on this campus have the financial means to attend here. None of my friends have jobs, not even my humble roommate.

Mitsy once told me she had stolen most of her wardrobe, but I don't think I ever fully believed her story. I can spot a thief a mile away, but I keep quiet. I don't think it is worth the risk of a confrontation. Who knows, maybe she is a thief, and I'm blind. Maybe wanna-be-rich kids with parents have stealing tendencies, too?

The students at this university dress in authentic designer clothes, don't complain about the costs of textbooks, have natural worries about ensuring the funds for their fraternity and sorority dues, and are everything opposite of who I am. Of course, most of them have parents who love and care for them. They don't fret over stretching $1.26, and I doubt any of them grasp the concept of having to hustle their way through life.

For as long as I can remember, I have worked for and earned everything I want, from clothes to the shoes on my feet and the shampoo in my shower. All I earned *without* wanting—*that* is what I struggle to forgive. No one's ever paid me to study.

Mitsy complains a lot about her annoying mom, always wanting to know who she is with, what she is doing, or if she has eaten anything. I'm not sure Mitsy knows how lucky she is to have a mother who cares. Catarina claimed to care for Nicole and me. I agree. She did care. She cared enough to screw up our childhood, just enough to cause the right amount of damage without getting caught.

Visiting Mrs. Gilly has helped me all morning. She gives me what some consider constructive criticism but coupled it with motherly advice. I appreciate this woman more than I can express. Since the day I met her, she has been a friend, an excellent listener, and an honest reflection of God's grace.

I hope every woman gets to meet someone like Mrs. Gilly at least once in their lifetime. Despite being on my own, experiencing the troubles attached to adulthood, this lady has shown me the strength of a true forgiver and the love of a mother.

Above all, every time we connect, she continues to plant the seed of God in my life. She gives me advice and the reassurance that if I ever need a place to run, her home is my home, too. Although she is a bit bossy with a twist of sassy, she is one of my favorite people.

Somehow, this woman, who was once a stranger, stepped into my life to do another woman's job. She has known me for a fraction of the time Catarina did, but I feel far greater love from Mrs. Gilly—the kind that is authentic and candid. For a moment, I forget what it feels like to be unloved.

This afternoon, Mrs. Gilly teaches me about notifying the IRS to ensure Catarina does not claim me on her income taxes. We share a cup of hot tea together, since I still can't handle the coffee, and she made an exceptionally healthy meal. Healthy and organic have never been part of my lifestyle.

When Nicole and I lived with Gina, the woman who birthed us, we ate whatever we could find. If it was all we had, we ate stale saltines and off-brand ketchup—possibly on a borrowed paper towel sitting on the stained carpet of a dressing room next to empty hangers and a slightly warped mirror.

During the brief time we lived with my grandmother, we ate whatever her hard-working hands prepared to nourish our bodies. We were grateful and never went to bed with an empty tummy when we lived with her.

When we moved in with Catarina, we ate whatever meal was served. There were no other options. Sometimes, Nicole would only drink the juice from the canned corn, claiming she didn't like corn kernels themselves.

Several years later, I discovered my sister loves corn. It's her favorite vegetable, but she chose to sacrifice that so we would both have enough to eat.

Nicole may be younger than me, but she is insultingly brilliant.

CHAPTER 32

It has been a while since they sent Nicole out of state to serve her time at a Federal Prison in Texas. Despite her youth, this isn't her first offense. Nicole took several falls for our foster mother. She must complete the majority of her sentence before she becomes eligible to appear before a parole board.

Despite concrete evidence Catarina coerced Nicole, the state offers no leniency for any crime committed. Catarina accepted a plea deal with no additional time served. Nicole chose not to cooperate with law enforcement, even refusing to speak to her public defender. The judge convicted and sentenced her to six years. I asked Nicole why she refused to cooperate, and she defensively told me if the police had believed her the first time, she wouldn't have a mile long rap sheet.

While imprisoned, Nicole's possession of a makeshift weapon resulted in an additional federal indictment. A deadly weapon inside a penitentiary carries a felony charge. Nicole no longer faced a six-year sentence, and parole was now a mirage. Not only would they keep my baby sister locked away for several more years, they transferred her from an in-state to an out-of-state facility.

She is now labeled as a violent offender. Nicole's guilt admission eliminated the need for legal representation, so no one fights for her now. And I can't visit her as easily when she's several states away.

I'm in grad school now but still struggle with feelings of remorse. Even after all this time and navigating the difficulty of talking to Catarina, I have done my best to persevere for Nicole. She is doing time for a crime she would have never voluntarily committed. I hate she is the one behind bars when it should be Catarina.

Even in the moments meant for vacation, Catarina always showed off her craftiness. During our trip to Disneyland, Catarina's idea of stealing from the small shops led to our expulsion from the theme park. The amount of secondhand embarrassment I felt was nauseating. I haven't returned since.

So many memories of that woman involve her forcing my sister and me into her corrupt schemes. Sometimes, I wonder how Nicole got to this point. Then, I remember who raised her—a broken system and an unprincipled human being who considered herself a mother.

I asked Catarina once why she had it in for us, and though I am not entirely sure she was being honest with me, her surprising response sounded truthful.

"Because of your mother! That's why! If you ever find her, you make sure to tell her I said that!!"

I can still recall her facial expressions and the switch in her demeanor.

She always seemed to flip like a light switch, from super friendly to caught in an emotional tornado. If I breathed wrong, everything would backfire. I tiptoed around my emotions to ensure I wouldn't step on Catarina's. Children should never have to make such accommodations for their parent.

Nicole has an upcoming hearing, and I can't attend because of final exams. There are certain people I would give my healthy organs to save. Nicole is one of them. But something as major as a college final exam, I cannot sacrifice.

My scholarship depends on my academic performance, and I will not risk losing it. I asked one professor to let me take the exam early, but he refused, in capital letters! With that type of response, I didn't bother asking any other professors.

Since I have little money to put into my sister's commissary account, I try my best to sell a thing or two from my closet every month to send to Nicole. Despite my gratitude for health and employment, two jobs prove inadequate in this economy. These days, it takes a two-income household to stay afloat and even then, it's barely nose-above-water.

My first job covers the expenses for my dorm, groceries to last me a week, and the phone bill. I miss that scholarship I had for my undergrad years. Now, I spend each penny I earn before I even see the check. My second job has come in handy with the expenses of everyday life, like my shampoo, since I finally upgraded from using bar soap to wash my hair.

I try to stay frugal, only shopping for second-hand clothes when I discover holes in my current wardrobe. My style now is "thrift store chic." I attempt to save any meager amount remaining for some source of transportation, even a bike!

Walking is my only option, but at least my legs are strong. If I need a ride anywhere and Mitsy is around, she usually takes me where I need to go. She has offered me her keys a handful of times to borrow her car for running errands, but I am too much of a rule follower. I've broken the law enough under duress from Catarina and prefer never to do so again.

Even though I'm in my twenties, I need a valid license to drive. Since no one ever taught me how, I enrolled in a driver's education course to learn. A warning or citation? I won't risk it. I never want to become like either of my foster parents, thinking I can get away with breaking the law.

When I meet someone new, they are often flabbergasted to find out I rarely drink alcohol, never smoked cigarettes, and always refuse experimentation with drugs. I don't plan to change soon, either. I don't want to find pleasure in a substance to fill the void. Addiction runs through my bloodline. Out of everything in the world that someone can become, an addict is at the bottom of my list.

Students legitimately enjoy their college years party hopping. My stressful life prevents me from joining them. It is tough juggling between trying to help Nicole, working two jobs, and attending grad school.

And sometimes, just having enough strength to be okay takes a lot.

Chapter 33

After debating changes to my graduate major, I decide to stick to psychology. I need to explore the factors shaping my identity and that of individuals like Catarina. Aside from spiritual depravity, her cruel actions and treatment of my sister and me suggest a psychological explanation.

Although, she also had an odd obsession with witchcraft. I don't know how much credence she gave it, but she talked about it constantly. If she spotted a black cat mysteriously walking across the street, she would claim her husband's ex-wife was casting spells on her. Then, other times, she would wind a thread-like material around her broom handle, expressing her belief in its power to "reverse the evil spirits."

One time, I saw a strange sort of evil come over Catarina—something felt different, and it was vile. She called out my name from the recliner. It was her favorite seat in her house. She showed me her phone screen, which displayed a photo of Santiago's newlywed relatives radiating happiness.

Then, in an instant, like rotten food in your digestive tract waiting to erupt from your system, she unleashed a torrent of hateful wishes upon the couple, cursing the couple's marriage, and declaring it would soon end. Something triggered inside me to watch Catarina with caution. She was not to be trifled with.

The crazy part of this entire thing was when I heard about the couple splitting up later on, it didn't surprise me. Family members remained clueless about their reasons for separating.

However, I understood the life-altering power of words. The Bible even mentions it in Proverbs 18:21. "Death and life are in the power of the tongue, and those who love it shall eat its fruits." Call it whatever you want, but I knew there was a kind of spiritual power in that experience, and it reminds me to be careful about getting carried away with my own words.

Learning about racial disparities in the juvenile system in class today was a great way to add guilt to my conscience. I feel culpable for the life Nicole is living. I'm burdened with regret that my sister will never experience a high school graduation ceremony. What appeared to be the best four years of school for me were the worst four years for Nicole.

She will never get to tell her future family she experienced being asked to prom or about the thrill of a senior graduation day. Nicole will spend her high school years in jail for a crime someone else forced her to commit as a child. Coexistence with Catarina eliminates options and opinions.

When you live with a narcissist, your thoughts are insignificant, and no matter how much you try, you will never achieve winning over their love. Frankly, you should never have to work for someone's attention, love, or affection. Especially not your parent!

I think that's why I love Mrs. Gilly so much. My respect for that woman is real. Nobody can attempt to cross her sideways around me because I will jump out of character for her. Though Mrs. Gilly's years are older than me, she is young at heart.

She looks so good for her age, but the light radiating from within is where her true beauty lies. Her love comes effortlessly. She embraces my fear of abandonment and gives me reassurance that soothes my soul. Her gray hair reflects her wisdom, and it comes in the rawest form possible.

Sylvia Gilly cares for me like her own. She doesn't even have to say it, because the way she treats me is sufficient.

After almost a year of exhausting labor, I worked enough shifts to buy my first car. It is nothing fancy, and I am not sure if it is reliable, but the ad on the flyer has an asking price of eleven hundred dollars. Today must be my lucky day, because I have exactly eleven crisp Benjamin Franklins. Snatching the flyer posted to the tree, I read the description of the vehicle while walking back to the dorms.

I have not had an appetite in several days, but today, they were serving hot, cheesy pizza, and I could not hold back. How many years has it been since I had a massive slice of pizza all to myself without feeling guilty or having to earn it one way or another?

That pizza tasted amazing. It felt even better when nobody shamed me for grabbing a second slice and then a third to take back to my dorm room. What a brilliant use of free will! I chose to attend a campus activity and ended up with free pizza. I finish the last bite inside my mouth of greasy cheese and a crunchy crust while punching in the numbers from the flyer.

"Hello." A male voice answers.

"Hi. Yes. I am calling about your car." My voice is squeakier than I intended.

"Yeah, I still got it. Come by the shop across from City Plaza Sporting Goods, and you'll see the car in the parking lot." I'm about to ask for directions, but he interrupts before I say anything more. "Go look at it if you want, and bring a mechanic if you need any confirmation it's not a lemon."

Before it gets too late, I want to look at the car. I was taking my time walking back to the dorms, but now I have to pick up the speed if I want to make it before the sun sinks too low on the horizon.

"Mitsy! Are you down to give me a ride to buy my first car?" I barge through the door, ready to beg if necessary.

"Sounds like an adventure to me. Let's go, girl!" Her smile says it all—she is truly happy for me. Mitsy is not the jealous type of friend. It may not be a car off the dealership lot, but it thrills her to be the friend taking me to buy my first car. She knows how much this means to me.

We arrive at City Plaza Sporting Goods, and the parking lot is empty, making it almost impossible not to see the car identical to the picture in the ad. I point toward a sunshine yellow Volkswagen Beetle, and Mitsy speeds up right in front of the car. Before she parks, I can barely keep myself in my seat. Exiting Mitsy's car, I know without a doubt this is the one. It looks nicer in person than it did in the photos, but I'm not complaining.

"Giiiiirrrlllll, this is niiiiiiiccccceeeee."

I still haven't figured out Mitsy's fake accent but I go with it. We walk around the used car that will soon extend the place I consider home. Before I redial the seller's number, I take a moment to envision my happy self picking my baby sister up from jail. I can't wait to write to her about this amazing moment. It's another win in my life without Catarina.

The last time I heard from my foster mother, being kind to her was not necessarily my top priority. I ripped her a new one, telling her how I truly felt because I had nothing left to lose. My sister has already lost enough.

I didn't owe Catarina an explanation, but I needed her to know how I felt. Have you ever wondered what it is like to lose your marbles? That's it right there—an intense feeling of spiraling down and unleashing it all with no regard for the abuser's reaction because you have hit your limit.

If you have ever felt that way, I can relate. Did that make me feel good? Did I feel better after saying those things? If someone had asked me either of those questions after hearing my conversation with Catarina, I would have been confident with my response. YES! Yes, it felt good to get those feelings off my chest, and yes, I felt better afterward.

A narcissist isn't always some mean ex-lover. Sometimes, it's a parent—the person who made a commitment to love you but miserably failed to do so. After bottling up inside what I wanted to say for years, I needed that release. When narcissists finally lose all control over their victims, there is no better feeling—a survivor taking a stand and then letting it all go.

CHAPTER 34

It seems I've spent my entire life searching for love and validation. As my second semester of grad school ends, my grade performance captures most of my attention. Love. Who has time for that?

If my parents were willing to even dish out the bare minimum to raise us, I would have taken it. As a little girl, I craved the slightest attention. I just wanted to someone to hear me. Though they seem identical, hearing and listening carry significantly different meanings. Anyone can hear a call for help, but who will stick around to listen and offer aid?

It's normal for people to run away from catastrophe the moment they see it. Chaos seems to follow me, no matter what I do. I hate to admit it, but I learned to thrive in it, too. Just look at my side of the dorm. If any licensed mental health professional walked into my room right now, they would recommend me for a psychiatric evaluation. My temporary home mimics my mental health.

I will soon have my own apartment, though, and I won't have to consider a campus dorm room my home anymore. Though I very much enjoyed it, it's time for the privacy of my own place.

Several months ago, I applied to the complex just a few blocks from the university. After many spoken prayers, I got the call as I clocked out from my shift at work. They approved my application. Maybe I can ask Mitsy to drive me over to check out the new place, since my perfect car isn't so perfect mechanically.

My phone's ringer is silenced, but the home screen lights up every few seconds in my peripheral vision. At first, I ignore it. But after the third flash, I grab the phone to see the notifications. Well, well, well, if it isn't Catarina Coyazo. Just like she rejected my call, I reject hers!

Remember when I said chaos follows me? This is precisely what I mean. Here I am several months later, almost a whole year of no contact with this psychopath. Then, when I think I am finally making progress toward healing, she reminds me why I see a therapist weekly. Catarina couldn't get through to me by calling, so now she sends text messages.

Narcissists flourish through victim response. I refuse to give her the satisfaction. Despite the temptation to address her, I ignore chaos and choose peace.

I love life right now. With everything progressing well, I'm happy. My new car has its quirks but gets me where I need to go—most of the time. I am passing all my college classes, and this weekend, I plan to daydream about my new apartment. Moving into your own place in this economy is a luxury.

"MITSY!! MITSY!!" I shout with urgency from across our shared dorm room.

"What could it possibly be now, Annie?" I sense a hint of annoyance in her voice.

No one enjoys being a bother. I actually care about other people's feelings, unlike Catarina. The only feelings she cares to validate are her own. If I ever had something important to share, I refrained from disclosing it to her.

"Oh, nothing, never mind."

"Stop, Annie! I have enough going on right now, and I asked like that because there is something always going on with you. So today, I may not have been the nicest when you called my name out. Sorry, dude."

Mitsy's comments fluster me, but I say nothing to her because it confirms my intrusive thoughts. *What if Mitsy is having a bad day, and here I am, always being a bother?* This is why asking someone for help terrifies me.

Anytime I asked Catarina for help, she would remind me why I shouldn't ask for help. The time I asked her to unlock the refrigerator so I could get some milk to eat cereal, her reaction made it clear. She spewed a choice expletive and glared at me.

"Do you think you can eat at any time of the day? Is my kitchen is a drive-thru restaurant? If the lock is on the fridge, don't you dare bother me!! You eat when I say!"

Or the time I asked her for five dollars to participate in a candy gram exchange at school.

"Do you think with the few dollars the state gives me for you that you deserve any of MY money?" An evil laugh often followed her questions.

Mitsy refocuses me, telling me to get ready to check out the new place. She may be rude sometimes, but I'm going to miss her. A few days ago, she confessed her plans to leave town once her boyfriend graduates from the military boot camp. It sounds like our time as roomies will end soon, anyway.

The apartment complex is only a short drive away. I probably could have walked it.

"I am so happy for you, Annie. If anyone in this world deserves happiness, it's you." Mitsy's expression flashes with anguish, and I know she tries to hold back tears. She pulls into the parking space in front of the leasing office, where a young lady greets us.

"Welcome! I'm Elsie Callahart." Elsie dresses to impress, wearing a hot pink blazer over a white summer dress. Her stilettos could gouge holes in the wooden floor. Gauging by her looks, the woman may even own the entire complex!

She is polite and explains she does not own the property, but she is the leasing agent. Her job is to show us the unit. This complex may not be the best, but it suits my needs. Residents can use any of the amenities offered, but the main one I care for is the laundry building. Accessible washers, dryers, and ironing tables? Yes, please and thank you! I have been doing my laundry at Mrs. Gilly's house since someone stole my clothes from the dorm laundry mat.

We walk into a unit with D-33 engraved on the front door. The moment we enter the apartment, I feel fraudulent. I'm not worthy of having a place of my own. Don't ask why. I have no clue.

I guess it doesn't feel fair to make it this far while the person I love the most sleeps on a dingy mattress behind steel bars with a roommate who looks like she wants to rip someone's face off. Guilt, grief, and unbelief overwhelm me at once. But at least opening up about the unhealed wounds is easier now that I've accepted they are not a reflection of weakness. They are the scars of my suffering—proof of pain and undeserved battles.

I shake them off and plaster what feels like a genuine smile on my face. Mitsy probably doesn't buy it, but Elsie will never know.

"I'll take it!" We return to the leasing office and start the paperwork.

I had no idea credit card debt screwed my credit until Elsie ran it through her system. I don't even have a credit card! When I found out my score was too low to be approved for a place to live, my expression said it all. I thought someone had stolen my identity, or maybe she had typed the information wrong. The system denied my application.

Mitsy generously offers to cosign for me. She's been rebuilding her credit, and it's decent now. They won't approve my application otherwise, so I agree. Just like that, plus a few signatures and a hefty deposit later, I lease my first solo home.

The car ride back is too quiet. Mitsy keeps adjusting the air like the cold can fix whatever is clawing at her chest. With both hands on the wheel, her eyes keep flicking toward me like she's trying to understand something deeper about the emotions she witnessed warring on my face back at the apartment.

We are a few blocks away from Mrs. Gilly's place when she just blurts it out.

"Why do you still believe in God?"

I don't even flinch or respond right away. I stare out the window and watch the streetlights blur past us.

"Because I've survived too much not to."

She exhales hard. That's what Mitsy does when she's annoyed or frustrated.

"But bad things keep happening to you. Over and over. Doesn't that make you question it? Doesn't that make you mad?"

She is literally missing the whole point. Since she says nothing after that, I keep talking.

"Of course I'm mad, Mitsy. I'm a freaking human!! You think I don't scream at God sometimes? You think I don't ask why God keeps picking me to suffer? But maybe, just maybe, God lets some of us break so we can learn how to rebuild ourselves with His help alone."

Mitsy remains quiet and uncomfortable, her focus on the road. But I'm not done.

"The day you can sit me down and prove that the sun shows up every morning on its own without a reminder, that the moon doesn't follow some kind of order knowing exactly where to be each night, that the ocean just takes a wild guess on how far to come in without drowning us all, that somehow none of this is God—that is the day I'll consider not saying my prayers before bed anymore."

Her hands tighten on the steering wheel. She looks like she doesn't know if she wants to hug me or drive off and never speak to me again. She mumbles that work called her in early so she can't take me all the way to Mrs. Gilly's house. Mitsy says it like she is apologizing, but it doesn't matter. I am grateful for the short ride.

I get out of the car, thanking Mitsy for driving me, and wave goodbye.

My shoes scrape the pavement as I walk. One block, two—heart pounding in that familiar rhythm of abandonment. When I reach the wall by Mrs. Gilly's, I don't think. I just move.

Throwing my arms over the wall, muscles aching from carrying too much grief, I pull myself up like I have something to prove to a God I can't see but still cry out to anyway. I scrape my knee without flinching. Pain is nothing new. I've bled before in places no one ever saw.

As I drop on the other side, breath catches in my throat. One thought slams through my head like thunder.

If He's trying to teach me something, I hope to God I will learn it soon.

Because I'm tired.

I'm tired of climbing.

I'm tired of being the girl who survives.

I still prayed that night. Not because I wanted to. Because I needed to. Because it's all I have left.

CHAPTER 35

It's been five more years and Nicole's prison release is today. She is getting out on good behavior after successfully completing half of her convicted sentence. I can't pick her up because my car won't make the drive on a highway for that many miles. Plus, I can't afford to take the time off work. If I miss a weekend of work to travel out of state to pick up Nicole, I would have to figure out a way to cover my rent due in three days plus the travel cost.

This is when a mother or father figure would be a blessing for us both. From the rent to other monthly bills, having to do everything on my own is financially stressful. Thankfully, I have no other mouths to feed. There is no way I could bring a child into this world right now. Abstinence is my only option until the right guy comes along.

Much transpired over the past five years. I graduated from college, but we held the ceremony virtually because of events beyond anyone's control. Every graduating student received two virtual invitation links for relatives or friends, so the system wouldn't bog down.

It's a shame after four long years of self-funded academic pursuits, virtual recognition before two of each student's family members is all I earned. I feel for people who had family to invite. Since I had no one, I gave my invite links to Mitsy.

The news that my graduating class was not having a traditional commencement gave me a secret thrill. I could log into my student account on my phone and watch my peers' photos in a PowerPoint slideshow from the solitude of my own space.

After finishing my college internship, I secured a fantastic position at the same company. If everything goes well, I will also complete grad school next year. I plan to use my degree to become a criminal mitigation specialist for the Innocence Project. It took several major changes before I committed to a specific field of study.

Social work was my interest, but I couldn't seem to separate my emotions from the professional setting. Almost every day, I went home heartbroken while I volunteered at the foster care agency. I wish I were making this up, but every woman I saw inside the facility visiting with their kids reminded me of my mother. Almost all of them. Maybe it's because so many of them looked like they chose drugs over their children. I am not judging anyone's physical appearance by any means, but an individual on drugs unmistakably betrays their condition.

Oh, and my friend, Mitsy! She is doing well. That crazy, but kind girl who never left my side is now long gone and married. I stay in touch with her by scrolling through social media. If I come across her posts, I smile, put a heart reaction on the post, and assume she is doing well. I discovered she was getting married on social media, the same with her pregnancy. I felt awful that I didn't know Mitsy was pregnant with Rylee almost until her due date. Lowkey, I didn't feel too bad.

I hardly have time for social media in between studying and my new job, so I wasn't keeping tabs on her posts. She told me she was expecting again during a video call. She never could keep a secret. The whole town might not know, but you better believe she'll tell her mother about it! So, if she ever swears not to tell anyone, just know that won't include her mom.

While Nicole was in prison, I tried my best to contact lawyers on her behalf. While inquiring about help for Nicole, I learned further details about Catarina's criminal activity. She used my social security number to take out credit cards under my name, had them shipped to her house, and maxed out every one of them. I am not sure what level of cruelty that falls under, but it's unbelievable!

What mother would ever think of doing such a thing to their own child? I am not sure why it surprised me. The credit cards were for places like children's clothing stores, and since I don't have children, that was easy to dispute. But several other cards were not as simple. I will not let it slide. I text her to let her know how foul I find her behavior, on top of it being illegal.

Catarina, you are such a miserable human. I have never felt the need to insult you with my words, but today is different. Believe me when I tell you this: I am nothing like you. My heart is not made like yours. I can't say what my mind thinks, but you're sick! I hope you understand and seek help. You seriously need clinical support. When you text me saying things like you never loved us. I don't understand you. I don't understand your level of ugliness. We were your kids! I am not that naïve little girl anymore, the one you used as a doormat to stomp all over. Why don't you help Nicole now? She is in that position because of you anyway, so why not offer to help? Oh, that's right, because you're no longer collecting a check for her, that's why! You never cared about anything other than getting that money! I want nothing to do with you ever again!!!

And immediately after I send the text dissertation, I block her number. I never want to hear from her again.

I am almost too embarrassed to talk about my issues with Catarina. Just thinking about my childhood makes my stomach nauseous. My phone screen lights up with an incoming text. The message is from an unsaved number. It's probably a scam. I read it anyway, just in case. The text message makes the few hairs on my arms stick straight up.

Your Lovely Little Sister Is Gonna Pay For It

I am tempted to delete the message, but I know I must keep it—just in case. This feels like one of Catarina's distorted games, a way for her to play with my mind again. If she only knows Nicole has been out of jail for the last few hours, she will use the information to inflict pain.

Chapter 36

I t's been almost a week since they released Nicole, but no word from her has come my way. I keep telling my delusional self maybe she forgot my number, even though she has been dialing the same number for over five years. Sleep hasn't been my friend in a few days, so that's also taking its toll on me. I have no time to feel depressed. I must get up and go to work. That has defined my life since I was seventeen. Work, school, work some more. Rinse and repeat.

I am saving to fix my car. My trusty yellow four-wheeled companion is staying put. I'll repair it rather than sell it. The cash would not make a difference either way with its list of mechanical problems, and I highly doubt my 1998 Volkswagen Beetle is worth the hassle.

For lunch today, I'm partaking of a cup of noodles. I love the simplicity of a meal requiring only water and a microwave. After my afternoon classes are over, my ideal plan is to enjoy a stress-free evening. But I'll check locally for Nicole while I eat. I need to make some calls.

Several phone conversations later reveal no one has seen Nicole at her mandated halfway house or anywhere in the surrounding area. The director of the transition program, who introduces herself as Becky Willis, tells me she has no records indicating Nicole checked into the facility. Now, since it's brought to their attention, the lady mentions Nicole violates a court-ordered agreement. I feel so guilty because I called, hoping to learn about Nicole's whereabouts. Instead, I think I got her in trouble.

I feel responsible because Ms. Willis informed me she has to notify the probation officer about Nicole. What kind of chaos have I created for my sister now? This is just peachy.

After endless hours of genuine effort in between lunch and classes to locate Nicole, nobody has heard from her. I feel sick to my stomach. She's not at any of the local hospitals or other businesses I came across in my search. Nothing. I'm so frightened, I burst into tears. A solid two minutes of ugly crying, too.

I grab my phone and open my photo app to admire the one that captures the innocent version of my baby sister and me. Our childhood photo won't lessen how much I miss her. I don't have to work tonight, so I think

I will drive around downtown to see if I can spot her anywhere.

After roaming up and down practically every street in the center of the city, I decide to head back to my apartment. No luck finding Nicole today.

I can't remember the last time I had a full night's rest, so tonight, I have to take this prescription to help me sleep. My primary care provider prescribed me a sleeping pill to ease some of my PTSD symptoms. Since I moved out of Catarina's house and Nicole disappeared, I started having panic attacks from the nightmares. These replayed scenarios are a compilation of traumatic memories that have turned into night terrors.

I don't take the medication often because it makes me feel drowsy and loopy. No wonder the label says CAUTION in such massive letters. Do not operate heavy machinery after consumption. Probably shouldn't try walking or making major decisions either.

The notification from my phone chimes loud enough to startle me. I jump out of my cozy accent chair and grab the device. It unlocks with a quick scan of my face. I can't believe what I see with my own eyes. If someone had told me this, there is no way I would have ever believed it, but the video leaves no doubt.

Each piece of my heart shatters a little more as I watch, unable to tear my eyes away from the screen. A skinny young woman smokes something that doesn't look like a cigarette. I don't know what drug she is doing, but the behavior is eerily similar to my mother's. But this woman is far too young to be my mother, despite the similarities in their appearance.

I pause the video playing on repeat, and call the number from which it came—my friend and former neighbor, Serena. She no longer lives here since accepting a job out of state. I'm confused that she, of all people, could have a video of my sister. I think of all connections between Serena and Nicole.

If our parents or foster parents had been responsible adults, maybe my sister wouldn't be as high as a kite right now. The Coyazos should have left us in the foster care system, giving us a chance at a couple who had genuine intentions of becoming nurturing parents. Catarina couldn't resist, though. Getting custody of us was her top priority for years.

I refocus on the ringing in my ear. Oh, yeah. I'm calling Serena. She knows where the video came from.

The phone rings a few more times, and I hear Serena's soft-spoken voice.

"Hello, Annie. I am so sorry."

Hearing her apologize makes me feel embarrassed. Why is she apologizing for sending me the video? Yeah, I get it's sad, but now I know something instead of nothing. Seriously, it's not even something she should say sorry for unless she provided her with the drugs. Maybe I'm just annoyed. Though it's probably not that big of a deal, I have a feeling any little thing anyone has to say about Nicole will make me crash out.

I look at my phone screen, and the call shows 00:43. We have been on this call for almost a minute in complete silence.

"You there, Annie?" I want to hang up and say my phone died, but I have to take this blow to the chest, too, I guess.

"Yeah, so how did you get that video?" I don't have time to beat around the bush.

Serena clears the mucus in her throat. "I took the video myself. Only because it's your little sister, the one you posted about on your Insta."

I reached out to my online friends for months, asking for help from anyone to let me know if they had seen or heard from Nicole. But nothing would have mentally prepared me to see raw footage of my sister following in our mother's footsteps. Nicole is barely in her twenties. She is too young to do this to herself! I want to hate Catarina with every fiber of my being and try to imagine possible ways I can retaliate for causing this.

Alone in my poorly lit room, staring at the wall, I think of ways to get revenge for the chaos she's caused in our lives. My mind races, but nothing sparks—no vengeful scheme, no elaborate plot, just a suffocating, lonely, dark feeling. God must have cut my heart from a different cloth. I find myself unable to hate Catarina Coyazo, however much I try. Caught in the mix of my realization, I am surprised at how tender my heart still is. Despite the pain Catarina and her husband inflicted upon my sister and me, there's no hatred inside.

I sometimes dislike being inherently nice. Despite the countless reasons that feed my frustrations toward Catarina or even my biological parents, I find myself unable to conceive even a single idea for revenge. Nothing I could imagine would bring her the pain she has inflicted upon Nicole and me.

My heart, unlike hers, is gentle and desires love, not vengeance—even if it is well-deserved. I have cried in solitude and have learned to vent in silence. Their actions have cut us both deeply, but living with them also taught me to trust people for who they *really* are. If someone shows their true nature, don't let it surprise you when they reveal it again.

I do not hate my parents for abandoning me. My thoughts don't even detest Catarina and Santiago Coyazo for treating us the way they did. I am where I am today because of it all. The pain, the trauma, and everything in between. I am grateful. Each wound these adults caused tells a story of survival, resilience, growth, and maturity. My heart will not seek vengeance. Even when it feels like it is entirely justifiable, I will choose kindness.

My shoulder and neck hurt from holding the phone up to my ear for the last two hours. Serena offers several resources to help navigate Nicole's substance abuse.

Nicole was good for a little while when we were younger, going to school, passing her classes, attending church, and being active in the community, but now everything is different. I appreciate Serena so much for this information, even if it's painful to hear. When she tells me the address where she suspects Nicole may be, I punch the details of the location into the GPS app on my phone.

I grab the first sweater I see, my wallet, and rush out the front door. Thankfully, my gas tank is mostly full. I need to hit the road now! I have never driven so many miles alone. Taking my barely working car is a considerable risk, especially when I have to drive on the highway for over four hundred miles with the remnants of a sleeping pill in my system.

Oh, well. May the good Lord take the wheel!

CHAPTER 37

The drive takes exactly five hours and fifty-eight minutes, consisting of an exhilarating stretch of anticipation. I drive through the small Arizona town and cruise each street in search of any sign of Nicole. My focus is not laser-sharp on the road. I rightfully deserve a citation for reckless driving.

I pull up to a red light and glance at the street corner on my right. Oh my gosh, my heart races! My mind can't process what my eyes see. Sweaty hands grip the steering wheel as the palpitations in my heart hit the inside of my chest cavity. With each internal boom, my stomach twists tighter inside. My mouth is so dry, it's tough to swallow.

I see her. A young girl. Lost perhaps? She looks passed out, halfway bent over, seemingly unaware of her surroundings. Unconscious and completely oblivious to everything. What the...my palm involuntarily plasters itself over my wide open mouth.

Could it be Nicole? I have no words. My mind is a whirlwind. What can you say or think when the person half-conscious on the side of the road is the person you love most? I feel embarrassed and ashamed of our parents, the system, and every adult in between. It's sickening to think of the number of grown-ups that failed us. How quickly things took a turn for the worse! I failed my baby sister.

For several years, I have missed my sister and prayed for her well-being while maintaining our only connection through letters and the occasional phone call. If I had the means to accept the charges, we would talk for a few minutes. I was happy to hear from her, despite the financial strain of the collect calls. What happened to that voice on the opposite end of the line?

After practically dragging Nicole into my car, I feel more lost than ever before. I'm clueless. Obviously, I did not think this through. I thought only of locating Nicole, and once I did, I'd figure it out. But I'm in over my head. I don't know how to take care of a drug addict. All I know is what I witnessed with our mother. I'm unfamiliar with the effects otherwise. I stay far away from drugs. What do I do now?

Nicole is asleep, so I am not concerned about her hurting herself or doing something dumb. She is lying on her side, spread out on the backseat of my car. My sister is so beautiful. Even if Nicole is going through a rough patch right now, she is still my beautiful baby sister. I stare at her through the sun visor mirror and admire her peaceful face.

In a split second, a wave of horror washes over me. The fact Nicole is in that state of mind, in my vehicle, terrifies me. I mean, I am her sister, but what if I wasn't? Something tragic could happen to Nicole, especially with all the news channels blasting these days about the rise in human trafficking. Unwarranted, intrusive thoughts overwhelm my mind. Anxiety fills me with questions about Nicole's safety, like where she's been and what she's been doing. This feels unjust. Since we were little girls, Nicole has gotten the short end of the stick.

I pull over as soon as I find a safe place. The clicking of the turn signal interrupts the silence in the car. I need a moment with Nicole. I reach my hand into the backseat, place it on my sister, and softly whisper to her still form.

"It's okay, Nicole. I have hope for you, even if you don't have any. Until you can find it yourself, I will keep hoping for you. I'll be strong for both of us."

This day is mentally exhausting. Never in my wildest dreams did I think I would be in this position. From web-searching different mental health facilities to learning about various insurance options available, I sure learned a lot today. I hope to develop a plan that will help Nicole. On top of worrying about aiding her, I have to worry about health insurance to cover her treatment.

I suppose I could bring Nicole home to live with me at my apartment. I know the risk I take housing a felon at a complex that strictly prohibits felons from residing on the premises. Felons can visit, but they cannot live there. It will only be a few days just until I get Nicole into a detox facility. There is no way they enforce this "no criminals allowed" rule because I'm confident the neighbor across the street has an actual criminal living with her!

That neighbor frequently reports the guy to the community watch page for domestic violence. She puts his mugshots on there with no shame, but returns home with him the same day. I spend a lot of time reading outside, so I pay attention to what happens with the neighbors.

Not too long ago, the same neighbors had the cops called to their apartment, and once again, they took the same guy away in cuffs. If there are any doubts regarding Nicole's presence, I will support her and highlight the numerous times the police had to intervene at the neighbors' place across the street because of domestic violence. At least Nicole isn't violent.

Or maybe I could look for a place that doesn't have rules that put my integrity in jeopardy.

Chapter 38

After the exhausting drive back home, pulling into the parking lot of my apartment complex grants me a glimpse of relief. We are finally home and safe. I do my best to wake Nicole up. A slight push against her right arm causes her to stir. Her eyes barely widen to narrow slits.

"Annie?" Her expression speaks volumes. She's clueless. "Annie. Oh, it's you, Sister."

I snap out of my daze as relief mingles with anger and frustration.

"Do you even know what just happened, *Nicole*?" She ignores me with an eye roll.

I disregard Nicole's attitude. If I upset her about anything, she may get out of the car using words I'd rather not hear. I swallow the chastisement on the tip of my tongue. It's not worth hurting Nicole's feelings. None of this is her fault. Not really.

I don't feel comfortable reaching out for help, but I have to set my pride aside. Someone will need to help me with Nicole. I can't do this alone. I try to do my best to locate our biological parents, but I have no money for a private investigator and no guidance to figure it out myself.

So, I call Chasity to see what she thinks. After all, if there is anyone who knows my situation, it's her, and she'll be able to help me navigate this mess.

"Annie Annie Ann!!!!" Chasity's cheerful greeting the moment our call connects draws me out of my stupor. "My goodness, I have missed you! How are you?"

I would love to chat extensively, but right now, I lack the time. I have to cut this short—sorry, Chas.

"I don't have much time right now, and my phone is about to die. Nicole needs help."

"No, Annie, I won't. You need to learn this time. Caring for another adult isn't your obligation. Your job is to take care of YOU! Annie!"

I can tell she's frustrated. She tells me anyone my age should do what college kids do. Not worry about having to raise my mother's grown child.

Chasity's words strangle my heart. She is right. It is not normal for me to worry about my sister like this. But I have nobody else to turn to. I'm desperate.

I thought I would never have to talk to Catarina again, but maybe she'll care enough to help this time. I punch in the memorized cell number. My call forwards to her voicemail, so I end the call and try again. The phone rings a few times, and then Catarina picks up.

"What do you want, Annie?"

With that type of greeting, she shuts me out before inviting me in. She couldn't even say, "Hi."

I don't know why I am surprised. This behavior is part of her nature. She thrives on feeling needed, and this is a prime situation for her to act dismissive. I'll bet that is precisely why she answered that way. Catarina knows the only reason I would ever call her is if I absolutely had to. Today, it is a necessity.

My need for support has me in a position where I feel bad for simply dialing Catarina's number. I don't hang up. I continue to listen to her. Once again, I take her blows to my chest. At least it's not physical this time.

Each insult serves as a painful reminder. If my parents cared, we wouldn't have to endure this. Nicole wouldn't even be in this mess!

I glance at my phone. This has gone on long enough. I have taken her nonsense, insults, and abuse for the last twenty-seven minutes and two seconds, and I can't endure any more. I regret giving her the satisfaction of once again belittling me. Why do I feel like a bother?

"Catarina, just shut up already!" An expletive escapes with my interruption even though I rarely use that language anymore.

I scream. What has gotten into me? I've officially lost it. My heart races knowing if I were nearby and had spoken like that in front of her, she would have knocked out every tooth inside my mouth.

"What did you just say? You piece of trash. I knew you would need me much quicker than I would ever need you." As Catarina spews hate, I picture her squirming, her cheeks turning red with anger. Her eyebrows naturally rise, and her eyes get this wide look.

It's kind of scary picturing it now, but I snap out of the imaginary facial expression reel, and I hang up the call. Who knows what I expected, but not that. I don't know why I continue to beg for a change from this woman.

As if that call wasn't enough, now I can't seem to find Nicole. She was just out here smoking a cigarette. I allow her to smoke as long as she doesn't bring the smell inside my place. I walk back inside my apartment, and Nicole is nowhere in sight. What is my life coming to? Terrible luck, I guess.

I call out Nicole's name.

Nobody responds, and the silence almost suffocates me. The emptiness inside my apartment is a lonely kind of quiet. I can't even afford to pay my electric bill now.

My bills were getting paid on time, and I was living just fine. I may have lived paycheck to paycheck, but I made it work. But now I'll be supporting Nicole financially, if I can find her. Everything in my life, especially my finances, is becoming a precarious balancing act.

This constant uphill battle feels exhausting. Nicole comes and goes at will, and I never seem to know where she is. It's been a few months now of the roller coaster that comes with caring for my sister.

A hard pounding sounds at my front door. For a second, I hope it's Nicole, but she knows not to knock. This complex is small, and if anyone sees her knocking on the door, my nosey neighbors will start asking questions. She can just walk in. I open the door without further hesitation.

"Hi, Annie. I hate to do this to you, but someone brought it to my attention, and now I have to ask if there is a felon living here? Do you have a boyfriend or something?"

The complex property manager, Lucy Sanders, exudes confidence as she stands before me. Her eyes scan my apartment. A man's presence here is her confident belief. All I want to know is who called her.

I deny the allegations. There isn't a "felon boyfriend" living here. I feel an instant jab of remorse at my fib. Withholding information is deceitful. Lucy's question about a man doesn't justify my silence concerning my sister being the actual felon. I continue to listen to the complaint Lucy received.

Apparently, someone made an anonymous tip reporting there was a felon living on the premises. The property manager has a duty to keep everyone paying rent safe, and that is why she is here, suspiciously examining every corner of my place. I go the extra mile to give my property manager, Lucy, the reassurance she needs.

I invite her in, and she obliges. She looks through the kitchen area, then peeps her head into the bathroom and pulls back the shower curtain.

"Well, if you had a man living here, he definitely smells girly." I chuckle at her mediocre joke.

She opens the closet in my hallway and then makes her way to the front door.

"Drop by anytime, Lucy!" I smile, but toss in a casual admission before she walks out the door. "My sister is going to be here a few days, and she's a felon."

She thinks I'm joking.

"A few days only, Annie. We don't allow long-term guests. And also, no felon boyfriends, please!" We both laugh at her last comment as she puts her notepad into her briefcase. Lucy closes the front door behind her on the way out.

Only one person would have done this—Catarina Coyazo. A few minutes later, I step outside to see if there is any sign of Nicole. I find none. No evidence at all.

"Nicole!!"
Silence.

CHAPTER 39

It has been another week this time since I heard from Nicole. I have no confirmation of her whereabouts, although I have my suspicions. I grab my keys and head out the door, an idea spawning in my mind.

Those on the street call it a "trap house." On my way there, I keep my eyes open for any sign of Nicole. I know about this place because I pulled her out of it only a few weeks before she got arrested again for not paying a court fee. Here I was, thinking she was doing okay. I'd seen no broken light bulbs or signs of paraphernalia, so I was hopeful. Praying she was not consuming drugs again. Otherwise, self-inflicted heartbreak awaits. If Nicole is back on drugs, then I have no choice but to kick her out. The thought of her returning to homelessness absolutely crushes me.

I wake up every morning and call the local hospitals within a 100-mile radius. They probably know me by name. I know that seems excessive, but Nicole told me she has walked further than that. One time, she was so desperate to find a way to consume, she went to a hospital, claiming she was in pain. Upon further questioning, she admitted to me she had visited all the local hospitals and urgent cares multiple times, requesting pain medication, until the staff realized her pattern.

An obvious struggle with addiction holds Nicole captive. For whatever reason, she felt compelled to resort to such meaningless tactics just to chase her high. I feel so bad for her.

I hear my phone ringing from the kitchen as I rinse the cup I used to drink water. Putting it upside down to air dry on the counter, I find my phone to see who's calling. It is an unknown number. I tap the red button on the phone screen with the bold wording, call rejected. Instantly, I regret not answering. It could have been Nicole. Dang it!

Sleep evades me for countless nights of tossing and turning. I can't seem to relax even if I want to. Anxiety is real. This hurts, even though I know an adult should handle their own decisions. I cannot make my heart offer an addict tough love. I don't enjoy receiving tough love myself, but it's far more difficult to be tough on Nicole. Maybe getting angry with her will make her listen when I warn her about the hole our mother dug and fell into repeatedly. I learned from watching her mistakes and don't want Nicole to plunge into the same abyss.

She may have given me birth, but I can't really think of her as my mother. A mother would never abandon her children, and a true mother would have gotten sober instead of allowing anyone to terminate her parental rights. Giving birth and getting someone pregnant are common abilities, but *true* parenting is what matters in raising a child. That is why I choose not to refer to my "birth giver" and the man who assisted in my conception as my parents. I know I'm not the only one who shares that sentiment.

Right now, though, my sister worries me. Who is she with? Has she eaten? I pray to God Nicole is safe. Listening to the news like I used to every morning causes immediate assumptions about Nicole's involvement in the crimes reported. Any time I watch the television, I can only hope the troubling local situations haven't caught up to her.

It is a painful realization when I think about the dangers often accompanying the drug-influenced lifestyle. I fear for Nicole's future. Even though I want to keep her safe, she needs professional help. I'm her college-aged sister. I'm not trained for that.

There is only so much I can do. I feel the burden, but I am at my wit's end. I am tired of doing it alone for so long. It's not Nicole's fault, but my sister needs help.

Chapter 40

Just great!! As if Catarina hasn't done enough, now she decided to sue me pro se in court. What in the world could she possibly try to sue me for? SHE IS THE CRIMINAL! It's one more frustration demanding my attention.

To make matters worse, an official served me the papers on my lunch break—at work. I explained everything to my manager, and it's going to be okay.

Still, Catarina takes the cake with this one. She doesn't even have the legal experience to represent herself in a lawsuit. I don't think she knows how to spell the word attorney without using spell check. I am not exaggerating.

One time, she sent me this long text about Nicole and how she had "mister meaners." I seriously had no clue what Catarina was talking about. I even had to Google search "Mister Meaner." Once I broke down and called her, she told me Nicole had caught *misdemeanor* charges. I muted the call to hide my hysterical hyena laughter.

She also doesn't know the difference between "your" and "you're." We are talking about basic spelling and grammar skills here.

Her lack of knowledge leaves me undaunted. I plan to retain an attorney to ensure I take the correct precautions and so a professional handles all matters legally. The lawsuit doesn't intimidate me because my faith in God is firm. He gives me the confidence to know everything will be okay.

A lawsuit for defamation of character, huh? Interesting. If that's the case, what's the statute of limitations for child abuse? Or for exploitation of a child?

I can't repay evil with evil. I have to *remain still* and remind myself God is in control, not me. One day, she will have to face God for her actions.

We all will.

My parents never peeled an orange for me as a child. It's okay. I didn't need them to do it, anyway. They should have for Nicole, though. She was just a baby!!

All my life, I've clapped so loudly for Nicole, secretly hoping she doesn't notice when others don't.

I remember a thought I typed into my phone not long after starting college. For my sister Nicole, I wouldn't just remove the rind from every orange—I'd peel an entire pomegranate.

Today is her birthday. I can't help but break down, knowing she is out in the streets. I am on my knees on the floor at the corner of my bed, my hands folded in front of me. Unspeakable pain surpasses all other pains. I miss my "family."

I had to delete social media because each happy family I scrolled by reopened the ache of all I lacked. It's nothing malicious. My entire life, I carried the wound of wishing our parents would have chosen us first.

They had their entire life to prioritize us, but they still didn't.

Why do I think I should call Catarina? Then, almost instantly, NO WAY! Not after she destroyed my sister's life and is now trying to sue me. She never even offered to help with so much as a roof over her head.

If I were to call Catarina hoping to rekindle the relationship, it would show her I am willing to stay through anything. She would take advantage of my humility and continue to *put* me through anything she felt inclined to do.

The last time I reached out to ask her for help with Nicole, she told me to deal with it. I needed to go ask my *real* family for help. I am thankful for Catarina's hurtful words. Because of them, I will never allow a human being to tell me twice they don't love me. There is no hope with the Coyazo family. Their love is not how I want to be loved for the rest of my life.

I search for those feelings of genuine affection, or maybe it's more than that. Deep down, I crave the unconditional love and joy of a family.

Instead of reaching out to Catarina, I remember her disrespect and tell myself it will be okay. I'll adjust to their absence. There is a lot of love to give in my heart. I may have lost someone who doesn't love me, but they lost two girls who would've given everything for them.

My other option is to find our parents. If I locate either our mother or our father, I will swallow every ounce of pain I feel and apologize, even though they don't deserve it. Maybe if I try to fix our relationship, Nicole and I will have something instead of nothing. After all, cold water feels warm when your hands are freezing. Maybe that works for hearts, too.

Instead of begging my mother and father back into our lives, I accept reality once again. Nicole and I may never know maternal love. I wholeheartedly believe everything happens for a reason. The whole "*you reap what you sow*" has a way of presenting itself in my life. What should have been the best years were, in return, the most traumatizing.

Narcissism amplifies its victim's internal struggles. But I learned to turn them into lessons. I survived. Catarina may have tested my resilience, but I turned out to be a great human being. Justice will even out in the end if it hasn't already for me.

I see every trial as a catalyst for growth and self-discovery. My entire life, I have desperately been searching for love. But now it hits me. I pray when I see an ambulance drive by. My smile brightens the day for strangers. I'm kind to my neighbors and wave to babies I see at the grocery store. I am love.

I still struggle with photos of my friends and their loving families, grappling with the feelings of emptiness, loneliness, and even profound sadness. They highlight the void in my life. Holidays like Mother's or Father's Day are unwanted reminders I have neither parental figure to celebrate.

I realize if Catarina, Santiago, or even our biological parents truly cared, they would have shielded us from this pain rather than allowing it. My heart yearns for a meaningful parent-child relationship, especially the love of a mother. My, oh my, does my heart wish it had that.

I don't want materialistic things. Heck, I use coupons to shop! But each night, I look up at the sky to make one wish. I wish, I wish, with all my heart, that somewhere out there, my mother is thinking of me and Nicole. Perhaps if I stopped wishing upon a star so much and prayed to the Creator of them instead, I would find what I seek.

CHAPTER 41

Nicole has been in the county jail for a month. Her sobriety is fantastic news—the best I've heard in weeks. Throughout nights that feel never-ending, I can't sleep for even a full hour. I toss and turn and wake up having a full-blown panic attack. Feelings of drowning pour over me, even though there is no water. My grip on reality is slipping. I am losing control.

With no choice but to seek psychiatric help for my mental health, I reach out to Ms. Gigi. This time, it is not for Nicole. I cannot take another sleepless night. The person in the mirror is unrecognizable.

I am only in my twenties, but goodness gracious! If I could see myself through someone else's eyes, I would know that person was going through it. The bags and dark circles under my eyes show evidence of sleep deprivation. Thankfully, I know where to find help.

I don't know what will happen next, but I can only take one hour at a time. Before therapy, I was familiar with the mantra of *taking it one day at a time*, but often, that felt too extreme and overwhelming. I opened up to my psychiatrist and told her I did not have the strength to focus on a whole day anymore. She encouraged me to break it down even further.

"Well, sweetie, then we take it one hour at a time."

These words have been transformative. One hour at a time? I can handle that.

Since I hope to find my parents one day, I have to start somewhere. Today, I choose to begin this journey. I want to end the cycle of abandonment that has plagued my life. Whether an adult chooses a substance or even another human being, anything other than raising their child, they forfeit their right to be called a parent.

I explicitly reserve the title of parent for those who show up. That's who should bail Nicole out and take her to get treatment. But, no. The burden weighs heavily on *my* shoulders. It's not too much of a problem for me, either. I just wish I had some help, that's all.

It feels like I have already done so much on my own, but hey, maybe surviving childhood by the grace of God and a flawed system just isn't enough.

Affordable investigators in the area are nonexistent. I need to pay my rent more than I need my parents' love. Ultimately, that is what this will boil down to. I can hire an attorney at the grand cost of $3,500 or a private investigator for half the amount. Either way, I can't afford those prices. Though they seem reasonable, I need every cent I earn to cover the cost of rent, school, and bills.

Yes, I had a full-ride scholarship for undergraduate school, but now I am in a graduate program. The cost of this degree is my load to bear. I also have student loan debt because that is how I survived school breaks.

I happily drove my 1998 Volkswagen until it gave out. After about 200k miles and several trips to the auto repair shop, the vehicle completely stopped turning on. No mechanic could salvage it or make repairs. According to everyone who inspected the buggy, I needed an entirely new engine to get it running again. It was a piece of junk. I sure miss my beetle, though.

I took out a small loan to add to my meager savings and bought another car with all the cash. At the time, it was the smartest thing to do to avoid a large bill like a full car payment.

Weeks prior, I noticed the car. I figured no one would drive such a horrid vehicle. I choked on my words, though, because I ended up buying what I could afford.

If I thought my 1998 Volkswagen Beetle was old, the car I drive now is ancient. I don't have the luxury of placing importance on the opinions of others. In this situation, the urgency of needing a source of transportation outweighed any external judgment. My 1976 Pontiac Grand Prix is growing on me, anyway. I ended up with a car even older than the Beetle because I had little funds saved for a rainy day.

Maybe I should have taken Catarina's advice a while back when my rent was due two weeks after getting laid off. For the first time in my entire adulthood, I didn't have enough to cover my expenses. When I broke down and asked Catarina for help, she asked if I had ever considered saving for a rainy day. Then, she pressured me to respond to her question. Clearly, if I was calling to ask for help, it meant I didn't have any money saved, but whatever. I admitted to my lack of savings.

Her bitter sarcasm makes the hairs on my arm stick up just thinking about it. "Sounds like it's raining, Annie. How does it feel?"

The thought of Catarina Coyazo makes me cringe, like when someone claws their long fingernails directly across a chalkboard. If I had taken Catarina's inconsiderate advice, I would have more money saved. I could have purchased a used car without the $1,000 loan. That is how I paid for the car in cash. I could have avoided the debt of that loan. It was a poor decision.

I did not consider reading the fine print when I took out the loan. An interest fee of 39% should be unconstitutional. I signed the paperwork because I told the loan officer I could only afford $40 a month. I was thrilled when she handed me the paperwork with an approval of $38.09 monthly. She obtained a cheaper payment than my original request.

The loan officer just failed to inform me of the interest. Upon signing the loan documentation for the following 60 months of payments, I would pay back a total of $2,285.40, including fees. My excuse was nobody taught me how to buy a car. It's not like I knew better.

Maybe I just feel sorry for myself for not having a dash of financial literacy.

CHAPTER 42

D esperate situations demand specific requests, not generic cries. If I am ever taken against my will, I will scream, "*Mom! Mom!! Mom!!!*" A *true* mother's instincts kick in for any child, not just for her own.

Ink on torn pieces of paper, ripped between the lines of trauma, grief, and genuine heartbreak, represents my past. They are a testament to my hard-fought journey. Struggling my entire life to survive, I have fought with sweat, tears, and immense pain to get to where I am.

I am almost finished with graduate school, and when I earn this degree, I hope it opens doors for a successful career. You would think after accumulating nearly a hundred grand in student loan debt, I would have three or four jobs. But I only have time for two while I focus on my schoolwork.

Although I feel the weight of hard work bearing down on me, I give myself credit for my work ethic. It is a powerful asset that continues to shape my success. I don't like to underestimate the value of kindness, but often, my heart is too considerate for my own good. Profound empathy for those facing hardship affects me.

Yesterday, for example, I sympathized with the unemployed. Those unable to work because of illness, disability, or other uncontrollable challenges. They display remarkable strength. It must be hard to feel excluded from daily privileges, like having a job.

It's sobering to contemplate hospitalized individuals battling the illnesses robbing them of daily life and work. I can't help my mind's wandering. And what about the elderly whose time spent working has come and gone? How do they fill their days afterward? It makes me miss Mrs. Gilly.

My absence from her has lasted long enough. I call Mrs. Gilly, wondering what she is up to this evening.

She rarely answers the phone like a normal person. "I'm so proud of you."

I like her greeting. She is the mother I wish I had while growing up. She rambles in defense of her son and daughter for the next two hours, as any mother should. I forget it is normal for a mother and daughter to disagree.

Sometimes, I get annoyed when she tells me little things her children are putting her through. If they could see their mother through my eyes, they would try to get it together!!! I know I am being dramatic. I needed to unburden myself.

"Mrs. Gilly, you know I'd be a perfect daughter if I had a mother like you."

I add a grin to my claim, since she knows my joke is far from the truth. I am sure Mrs. Gilly's kids know how great their mother is. My rant is over—unless Mrs. Gilly feels upset again about her daughter neglecting to wish her a good morning. Anyone who hurts this woman in any way is unintentionally hurting me, too.

I can't seem to understand the relationship Mrs. Gilly has with her children. How could I know something I have never experienced? I cherish her deeply. Her love sustains me through my self-doubt.

I accepted long ago she has her own children who have the privilege of calling her mother. She may not be my biological mother, but she's the most motherly person I know. I hope her children don't mind.

The unbreakable bond between a mother and her daughter is profoundly beautiful. Watching those interactions makes my palms sweaty and my heart palpitations almost visible on my chest—not with envy, but with yearning. Why envy fleeting beauty? No way!

If you have a mother with whom you can share every special moment, and even the more difficult occasions, cherish her. Someone out there prays every night to have anything close to that type of bond.

Nicole experienced no parental nurturing at all. She faced unimaginable challenges since the beginning of her life, which few people can fully comprehend. At least my mother was sober when she gave birth to me, but poor Nicole. She entered this world weighing barely three and a half pounds and struggling with the effects of the substances my mother consumed throughout the pregnancy.

It is a heartbreaking reality to think of a baby so tiny and vulnerable, struggling because of her mother's choices. While one woman prays for the ability to conceive a child, there is another woman forfeiting that privilege.

Addiction can ensnare anyone. I pray my story serves as a reminder to show grace. Those caught inside the trap of substance abuse often find themselves unable to give the care their child deserves. Unknowing, they subject an unborn baby to the repercussions of their choices, oblivious to the impact these challenges will have on that innocent life. I deeply sympathize with children whose mothers' struggles impede their own embracing of motherhood.

Mrs. Gilly invited me over earlier when we chatted, but I am too lazy to walk to her place. I know I could drive, but gas prices are outrageous right now.

I throw my body across my worn-out sofa, the metal prongs poking my back as an irritating reminder of my need to save my money. Maybe I should have called Mrs. Gilly and asked her to pick me up. My evening would have been more productive than scrolling through social media and lounging on the sofa.

I spend countless hours watching and rewatching this content creator I adore. Her videos normalize my feelings. She posts raw content that is not always meant to be funny or whatever, but her posts are a stark reminder there are other people I can relate to. She may not have my story, but her self-confidence is what I admire.

While scrolling through her page, I click the most recent video. Only uploaded three hours ago, it provides a sense of comfort.

She says something like, "Even if people treat me lame or do lame things to me, it doesn't make me a lame person." That's a solid truth. I allow it to sink deep into the garden of my heart and take root. I'll definitely want to water that later.

Chapter 43

As night falls, I'm tired of scrolling and move to my bed. Sleep eludes me, as usual, so I focus on reflecting. It's been a while since I've tried to locate my parents. If they only knew how much I still love them despite their absence in my life—even if they don't love me back. My entire existence, I pleaded in silence for their affection, like a loyal dog yearning for attention. I would have gladly barked, too. How ironic is that?

The day I realized I lacked something my friends had, I was in first grade. I was in Teacher Dory's class. We were working in pairs, and the teacher partnered me with this girl named Peyton. We were coloring family portraits when she asked an innocent question out of the blue.

"What does your daddy do for work?"

"I don't have one of those."

Her face registered shock at my answer. Apparently, that wasn't the response she anticipated.

I was maybe five or six. I didn't know what to tell her! It's a question that still upsets me, even years later. The memory bothers me because it was the first day my father broke my heart—before I'd even met him.

No child deserves to know what heartbreak feels like. I don't like that fathering means impregnating or inseminating, but mothering means exactly what it means. The roles of father and mother are so much more than the acts associated with getting pregnant and giving birth.

A father is supposed to be his daughter's first love, a safe harbor of protection from all that is horrible in this world. Bringing a child into this world should lead a mother to feed, nurture, and hold her child close to her heart, so there is no doubt in that little one's mind she holds value and worth.

But instead of all that, I endured a traumatic childhood with no inkling of the true nature of parenthood the way God designed it.

My broken heart stems not from fleeting puppy love. Any sort of romantic involvement would pale compared to the emotional wounds inflicted on me since birth. Instead, their absence has left an indelible mark on my core. Every single day, I carry that injury with me, filled with pain not worth explaining anymore. Regardless of how often I share the scars to try to heal them, I end up hurting more.

The last person I allowed to violate my boundaries was someone I considered a friend. I trusted her. But

I learned my lesson from our failed friendship. She posted a negative comment about me online. I am not confrontational, so it wasn't that big of a deal. Still, as my friend, she should've never made a public joke at my expense!!!

It seems people's cruelty comes out in spades while they hide behind a computer screen. I can pour my heart out with genuine authenticity, and somehow, someone will find a way to add a hateful remark. Even if I don't comprehend their reasoning, I try to remind myself to be compassionate. I can't be open to understanding someone if I've already decided not to listen to them.

I may never accept there are cruel people in this life. But sometimes, it's unavoidable. *Her mom tells her she is the greatest when she is mediocre at best.* My former friend thought posting that statement was a hilarious joke. Little did she know the joke was on her. I don't even have a mom. Where that came from, I still don't know because I thought we were friends!

I trusted her with my pain, and she offered me hers. She knew a lot about me, but didn't know it all. She didn't know my family dynamics, even though we had every class together in grad school. I shared some with her, but something inside me kept me from confiding my deepest vulnerabilities. When all the online stuff happened, it was obvious. She didn't hate me. It was herself she despised. She did her best to project her own insecurities onto me.

She met my attempts at friendly small talk with silence or rude comments. "How does it feel to be your parents' doormat?"

I must have needed a friend *that* badly, willing to take her bullying, so I didn't feel left out in class. Her snarky comments added fuel to my trauma. I had to get away from her.

In the end, the friendship was great for me. I learned not everyone who says they'll listen to you is your friend. Not everyone who stands in your corner wants to be there. Not everyone who congratulates you is genuinely rooting for you. And not everyone who tells you they're happy for you is actually happy for *you.* Read that again if you have to.

The termination of this friendship taught me to keep my dreams, secrets, and feelings sacred. I discovered, though, there is someone who knows them all intimately despite my hiding.

There is an ongoing trend of "meeting your younger self for coffee" so you can offer that inexperienced version some time-tested wisdom and maybe find a little healing along the way. I don't drink coffee, but today, I met Jesus for tea. The moment His eyes met mine, He wept. I asked Him why He cried and heard His answer almost audibly.

"Because seven years ago, you begged me to take you. Now, you pray for me to consume you."

A friend once asked why everything revolves around my faith in God. In my situation, it is straightforward. God is the only One who has made a difference in my life.

He stays when everyone else leaves and forgives me when I don't deserve it. He picked me up, held me, and never let go. Through the calm and the storm, God has been the only strength in my life. It took me years to figure it out. I have never been alone. He has been right there, right by my side, the entire time.

I feel God's tangible love wrap around me, His comforting presence gently reassuring me everything will be okay. While I have never seen God, I have felt him. I explain to my friends that to me, God is like the air I breathe. Without Him, I couldn't exist.

Obviously, I can't see the air around me, but I can feel it when it moves. The same is true of God. He is like the wind. Gentle and soothing most of the time. Fierce and wild as He aids in my most desperate trials.

There were times I had no idea how my paycheck would cover my bills and buy groceries in the same week, but I always seemed to have enough to meet my needs. That was God.

Or the time a doctor referred me to an oncologist because my body was presenting Leukemia-like symptoms, but the specialist claimed I was "as healthy as an ox." The oncologist shared my surprise that day. You should have seen the look on his face. We both knew that could have only been God.

When it is time to share your story and grow from your pain, you will find strength in everything you've endured. It takes courage to share, but it's important to write your pain. Pick up the pen and put your thoughts on paper. Pour out your feelings as the ink flows, and slowly heal as it dries. Maybe you are the one who needs to read this. If so, get up! Tell your story. Protect your narrative. It's yours to share.

And this is for anyone reading, never let bitterness take root.

I'll admit, I am still healing. My life's egregious facts and circumstances may not be for this world. No one wrapped them in a glitzy package with a tidy little bow.

As a kid, I stretched truths simply because of an internal desire to please those around me. Even if I didn't want to do something, I did it anyway. I always tiptoed around the emotions of others, even if they stomped on mine. It's hard to tell my story—these childhood atrocities—but I choose to do it anyway.

Out of every person depicted in the Bible, I unequivocally relate to Job. It's fitting to connect with a single biblical character, but precisely, he's the one God allowed the devil to destroy—literally HAVE AT HIM. God granted the enemy permission to devastate Job by any means necessary, taking his family, tormenting his body, annihilating anything and everything with one exception. He could not kill Job. I have endured incomprehensible trials, but they only remind me of God's power.

I have to be honest. When certain men were demolishing my innocence as a little girl, I wondered, "God, where are you?" But, amid the tears and human reaction, I realize He is a fair God and does not intervene with anyone's free will.

I do firmly believe those who violate children's innocence will face consequences. Frankly, having to appear before God for your actions sounds scarier than being sent to any maximum security prison.

Ignoring a manipulative woman's lies could have also prevented Catarina's abuse. But I could never find fault in a child whose actions result from a competent adult's wrongdoing.

Sometimes, the things we go through in life are because of self-inflicted wounds. But when evil people have free will to do evil things, they leave us searching for the purpose of our pain. Rather than allow it to destroy us, we find a way to release the bitterness and praise God in the midst of it all—just like Job.

CHAPTER 44

I f you're wondering if I found God inside a church or some happy place, that is far from the truth. God found me on the edge of a bed, fighting for my life, gasping for air as my body trembled at the reaction of consuming an entire bottle of medication. That's the ugly truth.

Living a fake life while trying to hide the pain. When someone asks me what I fear, I obviously can't tell them my biggest fear is becoming like my mother, so instead, I say spiders. *I'm afraid of spiders.*

During this tragic point of my life, I was fortunate to have built that village I mentioned. One of those friends is Alexandria. I will never forget how close we were, even though I kept so much of my pain hidden from her. The day I ceased communication, she morphed into detective mode. She even contacted my apartment manager to locate me.

After several days, she kept trying. Alexandria looked through my list of friends on social media and contacted a good friend of mine, Mercedes.

Alexandria's willingness to unearth my location will not go unnoticed.

She messaged Mercedes, a girl she had never met, and asked if she had heard from me. Alexandria assumed a connection between Mercedes and me because she comments on every post and every picture. Mercedes is that girl, always hyping up other women! Anyway, I came to find out Alexandria spent great effort trying to locate me, all to discover I was in a hospital bed fighting for my life. Mercedes told her what she had heard. That's all I know.

Once the hospital released me, Alexandria took me in. She fed me my first decent meal in days. I was on life's struggle bus. To regain stability, I sold nearly everything I owned. I lost my job due to frequent call-ins. My mental health was the closest it had ever been to its breaking point. I couldn't go to work because I couldn't get my depressed self out of bed. I parted ways with things that held sentimental value, but I had to do what was necessary to survive.

Alexandria never asked me questions. She opened up her home to me with loving arms. She was already undergoing her own trauma and battling a divorce, but this woman still found the strength to show kindness even when her world was falling apart.

Not only did Alexandria feed me and give me a safe place to rest, but she also gave me a job. I accepted the generous offer. Getting to know her and her family was special to me. When I had to move away to better myself, she understood how to help with that, too.

We have gone several months without speaking to each other, but each time we connect, it's like we never lost contact to begin with. Alexandria knew how to help me without me ever saying a word.

Are you wondering how I ended up in such a low place? My mother didn't have to be active in my life for me to carry pieces of the pain she felt. The thing is, I didn't take those pills because I wanted to stop living. I took them to escape reality. I am so thankful to be alive today because Nicole would be alone if I weren't.

If I were gone, she would have nobody to look up to. I catch myself saying I am alone, or Nicole doesn't have anyone—but she has me, and I have her. Despite lacking parents, we have each other.

Survival mode has been our constant since birth. Our parents taught us one thing without ever being present in our lives—how to survive. I didn't almost lose my life in my apartment that day because of my lack of survival skills. Even on my deathbed, I fought. I was not afraid to die. I was afraid to live.

It's been well over seven years since I tried to take my life. After all this time, I learned the message in that. I now know that day, I stopped trying to take matters into my own hands. I surrendered. The day

I turned to God is when my perspective changed for everything.

I no longer view my past as troubled. My future is no longer a worry. I began to live in the present and cherish my life, which was the authentic message—recognizing life is beautiful in the highs and lows. I tried to end it all that night in my apartment, feeling depressed, completely crushed, and lost because of past pain and future worries which were out of my control.

Now, I can focus on Nicole from a healthier place. The fact there is no way to save Nicole from her habits internally crushes my soul.

She didn't even earn a high school diploma. My baby sister has no life skills and little to no work ethic. All I can do is accept things are the way they are. Nicole has spent more time behind bars than alone in the outside world. I have hope it is not too late for Nicole to change her life.

She is still young and has a lot to live for. Nicole needs to fix her life. Her story is unfinished. I spoke to the attorney assigned to represent her case, Jack Meadow. A court-ordered psychiatric evaluation has kept Nicole detained at the county jail, but she is finally being released again today. The State ordered a mental health professional to evaluate and diagnose her.

I learned Nicole was homeless for several months after she lived with me. During that period, she resorted to the criminal-like tendencies she picked up from Catarina. They caught Nicole stealing a pack of Vienna sausages and a loaf of bread from a local store. She walked into a thrift store, put on some shoes, and ran out the door with a list of other misdemeanors.

When the psychiatrist completed her evaluation, the court notified Mr. Meadow. He called to inform me the court deemed Nicole incompetent.

Upon learning what the word "incompetent" means in legalese, I quickly search for the correctional facility's number to determine why they are releasing someone incompetent into the public when they should rehabilitate them! The frustration and anger inside me is enough to make my stomach churn.

Mr. Meadow made it very clear in the State we live, seeking mental health has to be voluntary. I can't force Nicole into rehab. She has to admit herself into a facility that offers treatment.

What if Nicole relapses? What if she doesn't agree to seek treatment? Someone who has loved a person with an addiction can understand the worry of all the "what-if's."

As much as I want to ignore the intrusive thoughts, I am only human.

I drive silently for seven miles, making my way downtown, where the county detention facility is located. No music. I even roll up the windows to prevent the outside noise from hurting my brain. Any sound right now will make me lose it. My clammy palm shifts the gear into park. I pull down the sun visor and wipe the sweat from my forehead, then get out of the car and make my way to the front door of the building. After successfully navigating numerous security checkpoints required to enter the building and even waiting almost an hour, I can finally hug my baby sister!!

Skin and bones. That's what I feel when I wrap my arms around Nicole. Her frail frame is a painful reminder to me I haven't quite been through everything. My sister never embraced the innocence of childhood. She didn't get the chance. So many outside influences robbed her of her teenage years, along with the opportunity to embrace the freedom of young adulthood. Maybe that is why I feel guilty every time I find joy in life.

When Nicole was in jail, she would always ask me the same question, no matter which direction our conversation was going.

"Sissy, what did you eat today?"

The knot in my throat chokes me as I share with her the details of my meal, like I did so many times. Even if all I had was trail mix, I still felt bad.

When they sentenced Nicole to prison for Catarina's orchestrated crimes, life seemed unfair. Somehow, being able to share little joys with my only sister was a constant guilt trip. Nicole is the only person I have ever loved while incarcerated, and let me tell you, it is extremely hard to do. I never knew the pleasure of scrounging up change to accept a collect call until it was my sister's.

When she first began serving her sentence, I devoted all of my free time to watching documentaries on how people treated the women in prison. That was a terrible thing I did to myself. My anxious thoughts consisted of Nicole. She wasn't in a place for children, but I knew she would be okay. Nicole knows how to survive, even if someone only gives her scraps. She's been doing that for a long time.

No more scraps now, though. We are heading home.

Once we're back at my apartment, I ask Nicole what she wants to eat for dinner, and her face immediately lights up at the suggestion of tacos. That is what we will eat tonight. I grab a plastic plate from the cabinet.

My plastic plate serves to chop up my veggies. I can rarely afford to eat meat that requires a chopping board, so the cost of spending even five dollars on an item I use once a year is not worth it right now. Chopping up the lettuce, I toss it into a plastic bowl. I reach over to grab the washed tomato and dice that, too. The garnish is ready to plate. I wash my plastic plate and remind myself I saved five bucks.

As I grate the cheese, Nicole reaches for a water bottle on the kitchen table, and I seize the opportunity to ask her about life in jail.

Nicole shrugs her shoulders. "I mean, I didn't have to worry if I was gonna wake up alive or not. I learned to appreciate a cold metal bed over a cardboard box. I was thankful to be off the streets, Annie."

My heart plummets into my stomach. I feel so bad for her. A mix of sorrow and helplessness swirls inside me.

I assemble our chicken tacos, and we settle onto my worn-out sofa because nothing is better than watching a good show while we enjoy our food. This moment we share feels so sacred. Watching Nicole enjoy her tacos brings a smile to my face.

Even after enduring everything life has thrown her way, she is still a little girl deep down. She loves the simple things in life and now we get to share these moments, like eating tacos and watching "The Little Rascals." Her movie choice surprises me. I've always enjoyed silly films, but it's just not one I expected

Nicole to choose. Given her history, I guess I am surprised she chose something so childlike.

If Nicole ever feels down, I pray she has the strength to remember these fleeting moments of happiness. Sitting here with Nicole doing normal sister things heals a part of my inner child.

My sister and I share the same story, just written in different fonts.

CHAPTER 45

Nicole was doing so well. She was making incredible progress, and I had hoped a new chapter in her life was about to begin.

While everything seemed to fall into place, Nicole returned to school and got her GED. That helped her get into a local trade school. I could see my sister returning. She looked happy to be alive, and her eyes no longer bore sadness.

Shortly after Nicole received her GED, she gifted me with the news she was expecting a baby. During this time, she constantly complained to me about her pain worsening after becoming pregnant. I encouraged her to see a doctor for her pain and anxiety.

Nicole suffered extensively behind bars, so chronic pain was just part of the laundry list of issues she dealt with. Being sentenced to maximum prison at a young age leaves little to no opportunity for self-defense. Nicole shared much with me about her life behind bars as a kid. Please don't take my word for it, but it feels like adults who do the unimaginable to children get a shorter sentence than someone who simply breaks into a home.

Nicole had her baby but then she relapsed. She had multiple stays at the county jail these past few months. Nicole doesn't even know how much her son has grown. My nephew's father, Uriah, has been doing everything he can to maintain full custody of the baby. Every hope I had for Nicole seems to rip from my chest in the blink of an eye.

Things appeared positive, and then they weren't. Nicole not only has me worrying about her, but now I'm concerned for her baby. Thankfully, my nephew's father is an active parent. He is one of her best decisions. Uriah does everything and anything for his baby boy!

The last call I got from Uriah was short. He revealed Nicole's pill abuse. Uriah told me a doctor prescribed Nicole medication for chronic pain, and she became addicted. I did not understand what he meant. I mean, everyone got prescribed meds, and if her doctor gave it to her, then it probably isn't unsafe to take. Following Uriah's call, I realized the situation's severity. Prescriptions did not differ from what she found on the streets.

I lack baby expertise, but I understand maternal absence significantly harms children. Just look at

Nicole and me. Our mother's absence especially took its toll on Nicole.

Several months later, when Uriah gave Nicole an ultimatum between getting sober or continuing down her current path, my sister chose the streets.

Once again, Nicole is in and out of jail. She disappears and doesn't contact me when she is high. I gave Nicole my word to never change my number. I know I should be angry with her, but I feel bad instead.

Okay, that's not entirely true. I am trying hard to convince myself I'm not angry at Nicole, but I am. I'm so angry, hurt, and disappointed that she is using her trauma as a crutch when it shouldn't be!

I don't know how things ended up this way, but the last I heard from Nicole, she seemed regretful about taking the pain medication the doctor prescribed her. In prison, they beat Nicole severely in prison for not wanting to engage in sexual activities. I never asked for details of the altercation, but I know another inmate seriously hurt her.

Doctors prescribed Nicole pain medication without knowing her full history. They gave a highly addictive medication to a person who was born prematurely because of an overdose of drugs in their system.

Lately, it seems as if Nicole has forgotten all about her son. I contacted Uriah to check in, except this time, I didn't get a chance to ask about Nicole. Uriah never missed a beat. My sister is missing.

Lengthy silence is unusual for her. Even the people she's been associating with lately haven't seen Nicole.

Earlier today, Uriah called the non-emergency number and filed a missing person report. He didn't tell me about it right away because he planned to come to my place to let me know face to face. Everyone knows how much I stress about my little sister. Any bad news relating to Nicole drives me into a panic attack. People say I worry a lot about my sister. It's true. I guess I do.

Every morning, I wake up at 5 am. I am not a fan of waking up early, but between the hours of 5 am and 6 am, I contact every local hospital. I search online for hospitals within my zip code and surrounding areas.

Once I have a list, I reach out to each medical facility individually. I know this drill well. While on hold, I dress and get ready for work. I ask each hospital the same question in hopes of a positive answer.

"Have you admitted anyone with the name Nicole, born in May?"

Blaming Catarina Coyazo and pointing the finger at her makes me feel good because I still have undesired feelings of anger toward her. I know I must forgive her. I push aside my pride and dial the number I know belongs to Catarina. She has kept the same cell number since 1952, and you can count on her never changing it.

After a few tries, a voice I recognize answers the call. But it's not Catarina's. I say nothing for a second, and then I hear a click. The call has ended! Within a few seconds, the screen illuminates with the caller ID displaying the name Catarina Coyazo.

"What do you want, Annie?" Her scratchy voice grates in my ear.

"Well, hello to you, too, Catarina. How are you?" I must remain calm to avoid any confrontation.

"No! No hello, Annie. Did I ask you how you're doing? Why are you asking me how I'm doing? Why do you have to be so nosey!" Catarina hisses at me, and I can almost smell her cigarette breath through the phone. "You know what is so crazy, Annie?"

I don't respond because her demented mind will twist my words no matter what I say.

"You live in torture every day, and I get to live in peace. Do you think Nicole is gonna change anytime soon? I know that's why you're calling."

I want to escape this problem by ending the call, but I listen to Catarina yap her sarcastic gums.

"And you know what else, Annie? The torture you have to live in every day is what you get, you little...!"

I interrupt her cruel comment to avoid listening to any more foul language than I have to.

"What torture, Catarina?"

"Oh, you don't know? Didn't you go to college? Don't you have a degree or whatever? Go figure it out yourself."

This is exactly why I am so glad to be out of her house. She doesn't even make sense most of the time. I redirect my question again.

"What do you mean, Catarina?"

"Tell me you don't worry nonstop about Nicole. I bet you are going crazy not knowing where she is. She chose this life as a junkie. Every breath I take, I hope you are the only one who has to deal with the stress!! And I mean it, too!" Catarina's shout rattles her loudest vocal chord. "That is your torture, Annie. Knowing your only sister you love so much is just like your mother, and you can't do anything about it!!!"

Maybe Catarina is right. Perhaps I can't do anything about Nicole. But at least I know the One who can, and He loves her even more than I do.

EPILOGUE

Remember these published words and hold on to the heartfelt message within this book.

In the moments when you feel weak, know that I, too, was once a hurt little girl.

Survivor of sexual abuse. Survivor of mental abuse. Survivor of physical abuse. Some find me excessive, others insufficient. However, this burden stems from years of self-reliance.

Through the trenches and by the grace of God, is the only way I made it through. That's all I can say.

I felt unappreciated and unnoticed my entire life, so I know how isolating it can sometimes feel. From the age of seventeen, managing on my own has been mostly overwhelming, but these emotions remind me of the challenges I've overcome. I gained strength from every experience and struggle I endured. It sounds daunting, but doing it on your own gets easier.

With time, these struggles shaped my understanding of myself and everyone around me.

For the first time, nobody told me what to do. For seventeen years of my life, I lived under the orders of surrounding adults. Leaving the Coyazos, though disruptive, ultimately gave me courage. That day, I no longer had to walk. I was strong enough to *run.* So I did precisely that. I ran. I ran so far. As far as I could, *away from her.*

At the moment, I struggle to find help for Nicole. I don't know where to turn for guidance on this one. Nicole is a mother. If she can't get it together for herself anymore, she needs to do it for her baby.

Though many experiences in my life left me feeling vulnerable and needing validation from others, I learned to seek the One who never failed me—God.

Our struggles do not define us. They are just fragments of our story. Together, we can gracefully carry our pieces of pain.

ABOUT THE AUTHOR

Brianne Audrey is an aspiring author nestled in the sun-drenched Southwest with her supportive fiancé, adventurous stepdaughter, and furry companions.

From her thoughts to pages, she shares her unwavering passion for storytelling. She invites readers to dive into her vivid imagination through stories that resonate or reflect both the beauty and the chaos of life. She writes to expose the trauma, break the silence, and give a voice to the pain they tried to bury. She writes for those who never felt heard, the ones who carry stories too heavy for small talk and too sacred to remain buried. Brianne is inspired by survival, the kind that is quiet, the kind most people overlook. She writes for the ones who get up, keep going, and choose to believe their voice still matters. For the broken. The betrayed. The silenced. The abandoned.

When she isn't crafting her narratives, you can find her cozily curled up on the couch with a psychological thriller, savoring precious moments with her loved ones, or traveling. She's no travel agent, but she loves the freedom in it. Her dream is to help others tell the stories they've never been able to put into words.

Brianne's faith is her anchor. It is the reason she creates, still believes in redemption, and trusts that even broken chapters can end in light. If you've ever felt like your pain is too complicated or your truth too messy, and if you find pieces of yourself in her pages, Brianne's prayer is for you to walk away a little more seen than when you first opened one of her novels.